BUTTERFLY MOON

Volume 72

Sun Tracks

An American Indian Literary Series

Series Editor

Ofelia Zepeda

Editorial Committee

Larry Evers

Joy Harjo

Geary Hobson

N. Scott Momaday

Irvin Morris

Simon J. Ortiz

Kate Shanley

Leslie Marmon Silko

Luci Tapahonso

BUTTERFLY MOON

Short Stories

ANITA ENDREZZE

THE UNIVERSITY OF
ARIZONA PRESS

TUCSON

I'd like to dedicate this book to my mother, Jean Heap, because she loves to read.

THE UNIVERSITY OF ARIZONA PRESS

© 2012 Anita Endrezze
All rights reserved

www.uapress.arizona.edu

Library of Congress Cataloging-in-Publication Data
Endrezze, Anita.
  Butterfly moon : short stories / Anita Endrezze.
    p. cm. — (Sun tracks : an American Indian literary series ; v. 72)
  ISBN 978-0-8165-0225-7 (pbk. : acid-free paper) 1. Short stories, American. 2. Indians of North
America—Fiction. 3. American fiction—Indian authors. 4. American fiction—20th century.
5. American fiction—21st century. I. Title.
  PS3555.N383B88 2012
  813'.54—dc23
                        2012001189

Publication of this book is made possible in part by the proceeds of a permanent endowment created
with the assistance of a Challenge Grant from the National Endowment for the Humanities, a federal
agency.

Manufactured in the United States of America on acid-free, archival-quality paper containing a minimum of 30% post-consumer waste and processed chlorine free.

17   16   15   14   13   12   6   5   4   3   2   1

CONTENTS

ACKNOWLEDGMENTS

Grateful acknowledgment is made to the editors of the following publications in which these stories first appeared.

"Belle's Gift" and "Where the Bones Are" in *Yellow Medicine Review,* Spring 2010.
"White Butterflies" in *Rosebud,* issue 21.
"On This Earth" published as "Ponies Gathering in the Dark" in *Ploughshares,* Spring 1994.
"Constellation of Angels" in *Reinventing the Enemy's Language: Contemporary Native Women's Writings of North America,* Gloria Bird and Joy Harjo, eds. (W.W. Norton, 1997).
"Simple Jay" in *Raven's Chronicles,* vol. 15, no. 2

I would also like to thank the staff of the University of Arizona Press, especially Kristen Buckles, and Lisa Williams. I appreciate your patience and careful attention to my manuscript.

BUTTERFLY MOON

ON THIS EARTH

The house was a forest remembering itself. The pine trees that held up the walls dreamed of stars dwelling in their needles. Jointed, branched, rooted, the trees still listened to the wind. The oak floors gleamed from the generations of human oils. Nails pierced the wooden beams, the iron remembering hands melting ores, hammering, straightening. When Iron sang, the humans slept uneasily, dreaming of spears, knives, the sharp edge of death.

Under the house, the ancient continent measured the journey of animals: giant beaver, tiny horses, elk, vast bears that clawed the horizon. Their bones lay in stone or were stone. And there was the memory of Ice Animals, walking into the sun, away from the mountains of ice and cold abysses.

Minerals and rocks shared memories. The tribe of Obsidian, those sharp-headed old ones, danced around the fire, singing about hunts before Iron. Flint swapped stories with Mica.

Long before this house was built, there was a marsh and beavers dammed the creek, gnawing down trees the size of night. The marsh became a meadow and sturdy wild horses ran into the thunder of their songs. They pulled grass with their strong teeth and fertilized the young pines with dung. Their foals stood weak-kneed under slivers of moon. The horses rode the back of life and died out, their species not to be seen again on this continent for hundreds of years. Trees grew over the meadow.

Once, the sky was full of burning spears. A tree caught on fire and burned an area around it before the rains drowned the flames, leaving a partially hollow log. Bears lived there, snuffling in their sleep. Years passed and the bears left. Moss weighed down the log. It collapsed and settled into the earth.

1

Later, a medicine man walked into the forest clearing. He heard the spirit bears growling and the horses calling. He smelled the clover odor of stars and knew this was the place for his sweat lodge.

He cleared the brush, pulling up plants with his old hands. He found rocks that had been carried by rivers of frozen water. They were born speckled, pitted, brindled, and solid. They were part of Grandmother Earth's medicine bag. The round ones he carried to the fire pit. He cut down saplings. He wove branches and made walls. He built a hut dark as the womb. He made a fire over the rocks. They blackened, hissed, and rolled. He tossed water over them and steam rose up.

This was his last sweat. His arms were muscled but the skin draped over the bones. While he sweated, he heard horses snorting. He heard the slap of beaver tails. He saw a woman wearing furs. She wore a necklace of a single mammoth tooth. She smiled at him and then disappeared. He saw a monstrous bird, wings wide as the wind.

When he finally crawled out of the lodge, the night was clear. He sensed some kind of structure around him. It was a house, he figured out. He walked among busy people who didn't see him. People were born and cradled in wood. They slept with wood touching the tops of their heads where their souls come out. They ate on tables of wood and stirred their pots with wooden spoons.

Then the people changed. The women's hair was curled. The men wore pieces of cloth to hold up their pants. And they cooked and cleaned and argued and loved until they opened the thick-planked door of death. They were carried away in wooden boxes.

Again, the women changed, wearing pants. The men wore cloth around their necks. They didn't use wood or clay vessels. They ate on something shiny and unbreakable. They didn't sleep on feathers or grass. They squirted poison on weeds and threw old furniture into the creek. They got sick a lot. They were forgetting their connection to the earth.

What astonished him was that they were all his children.

Their skins were pink, golden, brown, black. Their eyes were the colors of rocks: obsidian, slate, amber. Or the color of trees: green, yellow, brown. Some had sky eyes: blue or thunderclouds. Their hair was the color of iron, bear, fire.

These were his descendants. How it happened he didn't understand.

The vision faded. He looked around him with a start. He recalled why he was here. His people were dying. He needed a cure. The sickness didn't respond to his usual plant medicine. He needed a new medicine, one that would stop the darkness gathering in his people. A leaf, a root, a flower that would stop death.

He knelt in front of his pack and sorted through his personal items: a wooden comb, a length of rawhide for his hair, a blue rock. He found his flute and laid it down. He pulled out his medicine bundle from the pack. He unrolled it. Packets of herbs were neatly bound. In a small bag, he fingered a splinter of wood scorched by lightning. He could feel its heat. He used the splinter for lancing. He ran his hand across his forehead, wiping away sweat. His fingers were long with sensitive pads. He could touch a patient and know the illness and the remedy.

He set aside a bundle of dried goldenrod. It was good for bee stings. There were also packets of dried leaves, stems, barks, and roots. Stinging nettle roots were good for childbirth and headaches or the pains in the joints of old people. Finally, he found two packets he'd been looking for. Dried strawberry leaves for tea and willow twigs for fever. He felt too hot but he ignored it. They were counting on him.

He brewed tea. He would eat nothing. He would fast and sweat until he knew which plant would help his people. He felt power in this place. With every step he took, he felt the force of timeless stories. Every place was sacred on this earth.

Two moons ago, the Ute trader had arrived in their camp, bringing sickness. His granddaughters' eyes were swollen from tears. His grandsons were angry because they were scared. The men wanted to fight the sickness, but it was invisible. They laid down their weapons and died.

A baby died. Then an old man. Everyone had terrible sores on their bodies. Death took the young men and the women full of child.

He finished his tea and went back to sweat some more. Inside the lodge, the air was thick. He threw more water on the rocks. The steam roiled the air. His chest tightened. He was the People's last hope. He swayed, dizzy.

The heat rose like a bear. It enveloped him, crushing him. He clutched his chest and fell over, his head striking the stones. He didn't see the buffalo gathering in his darkness, their hooves heavy and powerful under a broken moon. Or the woman riding a horse; she caught up his soul and pulled him up behind her. He felt the wind in his hair and shouted with joy.

He forgot his life on earth.

Three nights later, a big storm blew in from the west. A tree fell down over the cold sweat lodge. It fell down on the bones of the old man, bones that mice carried away to gnaw on. Plants grew from the powdery bones. A forest grew up in the clearing.

As the centuries passed, men came with axes. A road snaked through the woods. One of his descendants built a house. While he was digging the foundation, he found a bone pipe. He took it over to his workbench and wiped it carefully with a rag. He put it to his lips and blew. He heard the sound of wind in the treetops, bears rumbling, horses neighing, elks trumpeting, geese honking. All of them were dreaming their last songs. And he heard an old man singing his love for his people.

CONSTELLATION OF ANGELS

Above the city, the constellation of angels glows. In the tribal dreams thick with broad leaves and clans of red fish and moons, the psychics sigh. They know we all come from lost tribes. Those who have lost their dreams, the world over, feel their eyes sealed with concrete and wake aching to see the natural world.

I emerge from the temple of the Dream-Walkers, standing with one cloudy hand on the dark red maples, breathing the lunar downpour of air.

I am a being from the Other Side, as you call it. But there are many sides and temples. Did not your Holy One say that his father's mansion had many rooms? I stand by the Temple of Reedy Rivers, its doors made of shifting sand and yellow canaries. There are many doors; I am one of them. My eyes can be as glittery as dragonfly wings. Or they can be as piercing as a cop's.

I step out and see the young woman who lives in the dark cracks of the city. Her lips are swollen; there is a black bubble of skin, the blood welling up and thickening. Her stomach is rounded with a new human hungry for life. She is remembering that her man hit her. She saw the bottle in one of his fists, and from the other fist, stars exploded. His long warrior's face was oily. She said she was sorry. She is a bearer of souls and fleshes out their bones with tiny veins and nerves that twitch at the sound of her heartbeat. She should never feel sorry. But she apologizes for his anger at life.

Mary is my Other, my special human. She would think of me as her guardian angel if she knew my palms touched her. The top of her head feels like sunshine.

Once, I divided my ancient self into grasses and wind. Long ago, I walked with the wind, which came from the lack of hooks and seams, mountains and buildings. Then humans made grass huts and ziggurats and forgot that the wind came from the Great Breath.

I watched over the humans with their thick thighs and golden arms. Or their skin dark as grapes or those with skins the color of almonds. Life on earth is heavy with burdens. Whenever I return to the Temple, into the nets of turquoise butterflies, I am astonished at my lightness.

Mary lives in a cold house. It has three rooms, but she lives in the kitchen. There she washes her underwear and hangs it over the backs of two chairs to dry. She has a table. Around it, Mary has piled newspapers and in the middle is a space where she places her older baby so she can be safe. Her man has big heavy boots that do not always care about what they step on. When he wears them, the floor shakes. She's a good mother. She takes care of him, too. She washes his clothes. She feeds him. And when he is drunk, she understands the logic of shadows and becomes one.

She's a chameleon; she wears her self-effacing camouflage the way a rose wears its thorns.

When he hit her he was thinking of another woman. He hadn't been home all night: he'd been with this other woman, and seeing Mary made him feel guilty. He hit her and felt better when she fell down. Her legs turned sideways to protect her stomach. He forgave her for existing. For a moment, though, seeing her curled on the floor, his leg ached to kick her.

The other woman had big brown nipples and small eyes the color of steel knives. He felt like he was being skinned alive when she looked at him over a shot of gin. But later, she moved her hips under him and she was very different than Mary, whose belly is baglike. The other woman had pretty hair. He couldn't remember her name. Maybe he'd see her again at that bar. Or maybe not.

He recalled the green army jacket she wore with nothing underneath so her breasts hung free, ready for grabbing. She'd worn a tight short skirt and black stilettos.

He'd seen her a few times before, smoking outside the bar, but she'd always ignored him. Last night, she'd been too drunk to remember that she'd rather be alone than be with him. Sometimes he got lucky that way with women.

He talks to himself a lot. He says "fuck" like a sacred mantra. Often it stretch-es out so long ... fuuuuuu ... he can't remember the reason for saying it. It's his favorite response to a broken shoelace, daylight when his head throbs, the car that almost clipped him as he staggered across the street, or his last smoke. It's as if he never got past his second of conception: fuck. He's not my responsibil-ity. Yet I put my hand on his head. His thoughts are like an onion made of ash: no center. His guardian angel avoids him, not liking the vermin-like feel of his thoughts. We have argued about this before. His angel has not given up, for we cannot do that, but he does not love the man. And the man needs love.

So I do what I can for Mary's sake.

My touch calms him.

He briefly remembers that his great-grandparents were healers. His ancestors coaxed corn from the desert. He remembers what he could've been. A healer himself. Before he was born, he wanted to be a doctor. But he forgot his goal in the temptations of life. He let one moment of drink turn into years of sodden indulgence. I see his soul: it has a rind on it, thick and knotted with lessons not learned.

Mary is a poet. She makes connections between her world and the Other Side. Yesterday, she thought: *I am one with the still stones and the woods. I could love a tree with its owl eyes. A tree is better at forgetting than I am. It has centuries of blue to reach out to. Who says that trees are soulless by having only wooden hearts?*

And who says that Mary is lessened by needing that man, the father of her children? Perhaps it is her lesson to be learned. Sometimes good comes out of bad. Or that is what she hopes.

I watch the young men on Second Avenue, smoking and waiting for the next needle. Something is broken in their chests. It is Life. Then I see the young women with their thin bodies, their deep bodies, their eyes stubborn and wasting. They need some man to cling to, the way rust clings to iron.

Mary doesn't drink or take drugs. She doesn't smoke. But she needs him like a balloon needs air to give it substance. That's her emptiness.

In the Temple, which is another frame of my existence, music has rainbows of sound, and cymbals are made of sunlight. There are roosters with feathers like red poppies, stones full of water, and salt candles that smell like the sea as it burns in a sunset. What is real is variety and we experience whatever we imagine, even water breathing. Sometimes there's a single stem of darkness. Heaven is life at its fullest possibilities.

Mary knows there's another world. I understand how she thinks. But, unlike myself, she is not *what* she thinks. It is not the difference between spirit and body. There is a vast difference between Mary of the Trees and the Mary of Apologies.

She gets ready to walk to the store. She tucks the baby into the nest of her arms so that the girl is resting on her unborn. She has a mental list: soap, milk, bread. Peace and quiet. She can smile at that.

The baby has a tooth that pokes out of her pink gums. She squirms in Mary's arms. It would be better for Mary if the baby stayed home. She glances at him.

He sits at the table, staring at his hands.

"Here," she says, handing him the baby. "I'll be back in a few minutes. I have to get our dinner."

"Can't you take her?" His head hurts and his ears feel like there's a big tree growing in each of them, roots digging into his brain.

"I can't carry her and the groceries. You can come with us. Or go yourself. Or you can watch her."

He rubs his face. "Why do I gotta do everything?" He sighs. "Okay, so what do I do with her?"

"Let her crawl around and don't let her put anything into her mouth." She hands him the toddler. "Can you do that?"

"Fuck." He looks at his daughter like she's an empty six-pack.

Mary watches him as he lowers his girl to the floor. She sits up and looks around with her big brown eyes. She sucks her thumb. Mary massages her lower back. He picks the dirt out from under a fingernail.

"Get some beer," he says.

"I don't have enough money."

He digs his thin wallet out of his back pocket and tosses her a five. "None of that lite shit." He fingers the remaining bills, wondering why he doesn't have more. Then he remembers the other woman.

Mary leaves.

At the store, she buys only as much as she can carry, which happens to be about the same as the amount of money she has. She feels a strange kind of comfort in that, thinking that sometimes life evens out.

At the checkout stand, the clerk speaks. "Your husband? He can't come in here no more. The boss told me to tell you that. He bothers the other customers. Please, tell him not to come anymore."

The clerk speaks very slowly, as if Mary is from another country, but Mary's ancestors have been here since the last Ice Age. Mary keeps her head down in embarrassment. She nods and picks up her bags of groceries and goes outside.

Another Dream-Walker comes to me, looking like a woman made out of white water lilies. She is the spirit helper of the baby in Mary.

Lily looks at me with her green eyes. Her pale face is oval with wide cheekbones and shell-pink lips.

"This baby is the paper shadows of birds. Her soul is ready to fly away. This baby is sick, like a hand without bones. No dancing will give it earthly wholeness. Her heart is a butterfly in a cage."

We are sad. I knew something was wrong. Lily touched my shoulder and stepped back through the door. It was good of her to tell me. Now she must prepare for the baby's arrival.

Mary stops. A startled look comes over her face. The bags fall from her hands. There is a terrible pain encircling her. She drops to her knees on the sidewalk. Her face is white, chalky white like the inner sky of an egg.

O White Shell Woman! Mary came from that clan, although no one in her family knows that. It was long ago, before the conquerors came from across the sea. Now she sees images flicker across her mind. . . . a woman carries a water jar on her head. The jar has a face like a baby.

The woman walks carefully, one foot at a time, but the feet change into seal flippers, and she trips. The jar falls, breaks, and a soul tumbles out. Shimmering, shimmering. Half-liquid with the glow of a star. The jar face is broken into tiny mirrors of eyes reflecting moons. The woman's hair coils into rivers of red.

The baby wants to float away. Hands wave gelatinous fingers, ears closed and flat as a rock. The mouth is shaped like a horse's hoof, the tongue an empty funnel. The baby's soul burns a spirit hole into the temple of the sky. But the baby is not ready to leave Mary's womb yet, even though the angels start to sing.

A constellation of angels welcomes her. They say: *Rest here, you with a face like an altar of innocent eyes. You are safe from the father who has a bottle for a god. Say goodbye to the mother who loved you. Here, we give you brightness and a crown of candles . . .*

On the sidewalk, the blood flowed and Mary lost her second little heart. She lay, dully hearing voices around her, the pain racking and cramping.

There was nothing I could do but press my spirit hand over her wildly beating heart and breathe the peace of doves over her head. It is hard to lose a baby, even one that is deformed. The baby was not seen but yet known to every cell of Mary's body. She hurt now, physically; later she'd feel her own heart breaking at the loss.

The ambulance wailed down the street, coming closer. People huddled around her. One woman cradled Mary's head.

The grocery clerk crossed her arms. "Don't they know they shouldn't drink when they're pregnant?"

A yeasty odor rose from the broken beer bottles sparkling in the late afternoon light.

A man shook his head. "Looks like she was all beat up. She from the Projects?"

"Oh, shut up," said the woman holding Mary. "Poor lady." She made soothing noises.

Another woman trembled. "She gonna lose that baby. Where's the goddam ambulance?"

The siren was getting louder. Mary felt like she was floating. She could see ashen-faced spirits reaching out their transparent hands, their black palms pulling out the dead fetus and unraveling the cord of life. The baby rose up and looked down on her mother.

She smiled, now beautiful and whole.

I took the child's feathery hand, and we walked up toward the temple of the Flower World. With each step, our eyes grew brighter and on our left, jade deer danced, butterfly cocoons rattling around their ankles, hooves flashing. From their antlers, clouds of colored birds scattered. On our right, two water drums shook the earth and flowers changed into white butterflies . . . symbols not of death, but of eternal life. Behind us, waves of stars unfolded from the sea. In front of us, holy trees set forth blossoms of wind. From all four directions, her ancestors danced in welcome.

The child shook free from my hand and joined the dancers. Her body twirled and leaped in birth.

In the other world, Mary was carried into the ambulance. I hovered over her, the faint sounds of sacred flutes fading into the screech of tires. There was the smell of asphalt, the astringent odor of medicine, and the bitter smell of blood flowering between her legs.

RAVEN'S MOON

1

"I have nothing to say to you," she said. Her dark eyes flashed.

He stirred uncomfortably on the hard chair. Everything in her house was hard edges. Except her body, he reminded himself. That was soft and luscious. He forced himself to be as tough as she was. He shrugged coldly. "Fine. I have nothing to say to you, either."

They stared at each other for a second, both faces closed and defiant and a little sad. Then Raven looked away. She sat stiffly, her back straight. Daylight streamed through the window panes, the light blue and wavy from the ancient glass. She'd imported the glass from a house demolished in the Old World. Her whole house, he thought bitterly, was built on ruins from somewhere else, as if she couldn't bear to live in something original and new. He sighed softly. Why couldn't she go with the times? It was an old argument.

He got up. "I'll take my stuff as soon as I can make arrangements."

Her shoulders relaxed a bit. Her voice softened. "I know it may take awhile to find someone to help you. Hey! What about Zorro? He's got that pickup."

Miguel smiled. Zorro's red pickup was held together by duct tape and spit and a few old spells. He shrugged. "Maybe. He's kinda busy right now."

She looked at him sharply. "Why? What's he up to?"

"The usual." He bit off the words, aware that Zorro was *his* friend, not *theirs*. When a couple broke up, they split from their friends, too. He wanted to snap that it was none of her business *now*.

Miguel stood up. The light cut his cheekbones. A strip of darkness hid his eyes. *Brujo,* she thought. *Brujo of my heart.* She flinched and then forced herself to be strong.

11

"He better not try to make water out of sand again."

He shook his head. "He only made mud, chica." He barked a laugh. "You know Zorro is pretty bad at whatever he does."

"Well, he did a good job with that spell for calming whirlwinds."

"Hmm." He nodded. Zorro did have a knack for the air elements. "But I wouldn't exactly say he *calmed* it." Zorro had brought the dust devil to its knees, and it swore allegiance to him. The devil's pale eyes spun in its sockets. It had no voice, but dust spoke a primeval tongue. Mica sparkled and the grainy sounds that came from the wind's center were angry. Zorro kept it in a red-painted box sealed with a strip of scalded lizard skin. The box hummed quietly among other curious objects in Zorro's study: Yaqui cloth wrapped around old turtle bones, a black stone that fell from the sky, pieces of lightning-struck sand that looked like twisted mandrake root, and scraps of useless spells written in animal blood on aged parchments stuck on a wickedly sharp spindle.

Raven knew they were through. She *knew* it in her bones. The Sacred Mother Moon had told her so. *Your time is done.* She'd felt his love unraveling like moonlight at dawn. The differences between them, the warring that attracted and repelled her, had become tiresome. He liked the modern world. Well, he would. He was a new brujo. Only a hundred years old. But that was not her concern anymore. No matter that he was handsome, with his dark blond hair and gray eyes in an olive-skinned face, his lean body and tight muscles. No matter that she'd taken him under her wing, teaching him things his First Teacher, Anna, had neglected. She knew why Anna and he had never gotten around to casting dark syllables and words filled with light: Anna had spent too much time in bed with Miguel. Raven gritted her teeth. She was done with him. She would soon forget him . . . and Anna. Anna, from her first Circle, a woman who had been her best friend, almost a sister, really. Anna, who had betrayed her many times through the centuries. Perhaps, even now, Anna was weaving a spell. Maybe it was not the full moon that spoke, but the dark side of the crescent: Anna's spiky enchantments.

But no matter, she thought. Anna could have him again if she wanted. Salt Snake had initiated Miguel but it was Anna, with her blue eyes and pale skin, who had taken him into the female mysteries. Only a witch could do that, one with Anna's talents. No man would understand how to call the moon down into a lover's heart until it glowed. Brujos knew only the hot passion of the sun. Passion that burned itself out all too soon; it was better to end it, she thought, while her heart was whole.

Miguel picked up his coat from the back of the chair and turned to go. "I'll call you," he said. He didn't look at her but just walked out the door, down the twisting hallway, and out the front door. It opened into a courtyard of flowering rhododendrons, their heavy, blood-red petals pooling onto the bricks. He tried to whistle nonchalantly, but his throat constricted.

He'd go visit Zorro.

Raven paced her study, eyeing the casting table dusted with failed spells and crumbled vocals. An old-fashioned ink pot was placed haphazardly on top of a portfolio of drawings of extinct plants. Although the pot threatened, quite persistently, that it would fall over at any minute, she ignored its tinny voice. It had been empty of ink ever since she'd stolen it from that officious priest in 1647. He'd recorded her name in his church census against her protests. No witch likes to be noted by those who wore the cross like a sword. She'd seen enough of her friends disappearing during the Inquisition, and some of them had not even been of the Old Religion. It had been enough that they were female.

Her hand wavered over a small cedar box. It contained the penis of a crusader, the one who had raped her. She lifted the box and shook it, liking the small rattle of his manhood. She shrugged. That was ancient history. She picked up a geode that had been artfully split in half, the stone egg cracked open to reveal an earth spell. She hefted it in one hand. It was solid and full of memories of fire and cooling and mountains worn down to meadows.

How she loved this quiet room with the feeling of the Old World. After centuries of wandering, of leaving towns where people had begun to be suspicious of her, of fleeing the Burning Time, she needed this sense of permanence, these links to the past. Even if it was all an illusion. There was nothing in this life that was unchangeable, not even love. Especially love.

This was her life now. Alone with her books and spells and black feathers. It was the way it should be. A witch, a woman of the Old Ways, really shouldn't fall in love, she told herself. It limits her. It sets conditions for her daily existence. It demanded that she divide her attention from her healing arts to the needs of a man. Even if he was a fellow practitioner of the Old Ways, it was inevitable that there would be grievous inequalities. She was tired of teaching him. She was tired of his youth and innocence. Or ignorance. She was tired of being so ancient and beautiful. Someone as old as she should look like the outside of a geode, she thought, somewhat seriously.

The mirror next to the armoire clearly showed her black hair, her full lips, the high cheekbones. She'd forgotten her ethnic heritage. Probably part Egyptian, a bit of the Nordic raiders who oared their long boats all the way down the Danube River to its mouth in the Black Sea, and part Indian from a wandering tribe of ancient Sanskrit-speaking women who wore bangles on their ankles. It mattered only because some spells spoke more strongly to those whose mothers came from places close to a spell's origins. Her finger trailed a line in the dust as she walked along the table and wondered what her life would be like without a man. The same as always, she reminded herself in a forgotten language. The dust whirled up, glittering, and caressed her lips with meaning.

2

Miguel slouched in Zorro's living room on an old sofa the color of oatmeal. It was the only bland thing in the room. A red and black Navaho rug hung from one wall, while boldly colored art shrines filled every shelf. Zorro was an artist as well as a chef. He made shrines out of old license plates, crates, hollowed-out TV sets, tin cans, and cigar boxes. The shrines were dedicated to his former girlfriends, or to deities he made up, such as the Goddess of Lost Socks, or the God of Rotten Intentions, and to animals he loved, chiefly his namesake, the Fox. *Kawis* in Yaqui.

He rolled a homemade cigarette and eyed Miguel. "So it's over, *jefe?*" Although both he and Miguel were half Yaqui, a tribe from northern Mexico and parts of the Southwest, they couldn't have looked less alike. Zorro's hair was blue-black and his eyes were obsidian. His was a stocky build, with muscular shoulders and narrow hips. Both had become witches in the 1800s in Sonora after undergoing not only rigid training, but a descent into a cave filled with snakes. They'd been high on *tebwi,* the hallucinogenic flower of the datura plant. Their Master Brujo was the famed Rarámuri Salt Snake, a man who had been alive since the preconquest days. He'd mixed the sacred herbs and called forth the flickering tongues of the spirit snakes to whisper secrets into his initiates' ears. They became witches, or *yee sisivomem,* sorcerers in Yaqui, because of their mothers' witch heritage and because Mama Mecha, the Woman Moon Spirit, wished it so.

Miguel was the son of a Yaqui servant woman and a white rancher. Zorro was the child of a Yaqui man and a Seri woman who was part French. They'd traveled north, following the railroad track, escaping the *federales,* who were rounding up Yaquis and selling them to the hemp plantations south of Mexico City.

They rented a small house in San Diego.

One weekend, they traveled down to Tijuana and met Raven, where she was making her living as a potter, firing up kilns so hot earth transformed into containers for water. It was in the 1920s and she had a lover, a man who hotfooted it over the border selling bathtub hooch. Miguel had eyed her from the safe distance of unavailability and was smitten at once. She'd seen the fire in his eyes but was distracted by her lover's hands shaping the clay of her body. Miguel said adios and headed back over the border with his sidekick, Zorro.

They moved to Los Angeles and later moved north again, reversing the Native migration pattern. They finally settled in a town near Seattle, finding work in the city as sales clerks or bartenders or in the old-growth woods as lumberjacks. Zorro had been mumbling lately about moving again. Maybe south. Away from the damp fogs that made his spells stick together or mildew.

Raven had shown up one snowy morning a year ago, homing in on their beacons of magic. She'd merely crooked a finger at Miguel and he'd followed her home, much to Zorro's disgust.

Miguel nodded. "It's over." He sniffed the air. Zorro's cigarette smelled like horse manure. He wrinkled his nose. "Disgusting stuff."

"You know, I gotta have my air." Zorro squinted through the rancid smoke. "You got your water, I got my air, even if it's burning."

Miguel was a water element witch. He loved being in rainy Seattle, where he swam his way to his car, taking gulps of heavy fog into his lungs, and exhaling small clouds of dew. For a desert Indian, Miguel was odd. He put his feet up on the coffee table. "But I'm thinking I can get her back. Question is: do I want to?"

Zorro sat up. His eyebrows shot up. "Get her back? *Get her back?* Are you loco, hermano?" His voice rose to a girlish squeak. "She's fire and you're water, and you know what that makes? Steam, steam, you idiot! I warned you about her. Remember?"

Miguel laughed softly. "Sí, I remember."

Zorro smirked. "What am I saying? Balls don't have ears." He grabbed his crotch and cackled, his laugh turning into a hacking cough.

Miguel waited until Zorro gained his breath. "Even witches can die." He pointed his chin at the smoldering cigarette in Zorro's hand.

"Nah." Zorro shook his head. "It'll take more than this to knock me off." He waved his cigarette, ash sprinkling his clothes. "But you . . . you will kill yourself over this woman." He snorted. "This Bird Woman who's likely to peck you to death."

Raven came from the clan of Raven from a forgotten tribal society. But her element wasn't air; it was fire, that transformative process that used air to create and kill. Like all Ravens, they dined on fallen warriors' battle lust and dreams of honor and loot. The clan made spells from the flames of strong emotions. They never lacked for raw materials.

Miguel sighed. "She's a strong woman," he agreed. "But I did love her."

"Did?"

"She's hard to live with, so intense. Everything is a crisis. She got mad if I didn't enunciate my spells clearly. She got mad if I turned on my music too loud. She said I was stupid for not learning Etruscan. And why should I learn it? No one speaks it anymore!" He shook his head. "You're right, amigo. She's trouble. But . . ."

Zorro groaned.

"But," continued Miguel, "I did find her fascinating. Still do. Even so." He paused and then continued softly, "I don't think I want her back."

Zorro twisted around to face his friend. "Good—and besides, you couldn't get her back even if you wanted. She's one tough armadillo." Zorro picked up his guitar and softly strummed a few chords.

Miguel was quiet for awhile. He wasn't sure what he wanted. It was a challenge to him, though. *Could* he get her back if he wanted to? He scratched his wrist where an old spell had burned its bone-lick into his own bone. He pursed his lips. "But . . . it might be fun to try."

Zorro groaned again. "You're one sick son of a *perra*." He laid the guitar aside and scratched his chin. "But then, you are from the Coyote clan." He shook his head. "I see nothing but sorrow ahead of you, my friend."

Miguel shrugged. "Might not be my sorrow."

His friend frowned. "What are you saying?"

"Maybe it's time for someone to teach Raven a lesson. You just don't throw people away when you're through with them."

Zorro was speechless. His mouth opened and closed. He shook his head.

Miguel added, "And just to make it interesting, I'm going commando."

Zorro found his voice. "You mean . . . no spells? Just . . ." His voice trailed off. He couldn't imagine what his friend was thinking of.

Miguel nodded. "No spells. Just my own natural charm. She won't be expecting that. And there will be no shimmers of glamour, no magic she can sniff out." He rubbed his hands together and grinned. "I'll blindside her. She'll never know what hit her. I'll make her beg to take me back, and then I'll walk away." He snapped his fingers. "Just like that."

Zorro stared at him. "You poor deluded fool."

"I have a plan. Sort of."

"What can I say, amigo?" Zorro shook his head. "You're an idiot."

As Miguel walked out to his car, he wondered if Zorro was right.

3

He stood in front of her door. It was the next day and it was a rainy afternoon. Early summer and the air glistened with liquid sunshine. Under one arm, he tucked an old shoebox. He rang the bell and waited.

In a few minutes he heard her on the other side and waved at the peephole. "It's me," he said.

The door opened. Raven was wearing a long black skirt and a turquoise blouse that made him catch his breath. The blouse was tight. A silver necklace dangled in her cleavage. *Get a grip,* he told himself. *You're over her.*

"Hi. I'm just stopping by to tell you that me and Zorro will be here about ten tomorrow morning."

She tilted her head. "You could've phoned."

He pretended to remember something suddenly. "Oh! Well, yeah, but I brought this too." He shook the box. She eyed it.

"What is it?" Her voice was bored.

"See, I'm moving back into my old room at Zorro's."

"Of course." She leaned against the door jamb and crossed her arms over her chest.

"I found this." He held out the box.

She reached for it automatically. He snatched it back. "It was in my old chest. The one from Sonora. I'm trying to tidy the room up."

She looked a little less annoyed. Maybe even curious.

Trap baited, he told himself, holding back a grin. "But I can't give it to you unless you promise to hold your temper."

She straightened up and narrowed her eyes. "What's that supposed to mean?"

"No throwing sparks at my crotch. No burning my eyebrows, like that time last summer." He allowed himself a smile. "You have to behave, sweetheart."

"Don't call me that." Her jaw tightened. "Look, I don't want to play any of your games. Go home." She turned to go.

"The reason you'll get mad is that this belonged to . . . Anna."

She stopped, half turned away from him. He held his breath. Slowly, she turned around.

"What did you say?"

He shook the box. An object rolled. "This belonged to Anna. I know I'm forbidden to mention her name, but I kind of wanted to know what it is."

Trap set.

She took a deep breath.

He pivoted on his heel and started to walk away, saying over his shoulder, "And I don't have to play your games, either, sweetheart. I just thought you might like to see it before I sell it."

"Wait!"

He stopped, turned around, and stepped back toward her.

17

Her face was rigid. "Let me see it."

"Promise first." He was enjoying this. She gritted her teeth.

"If you're that afraid of me, I promise not to hurt you."

He laughed. "I'm not afraid of you *now*, sweetheart. I'm just trying to avoid a scene. Your little temper tantrums are too juvenile." He added, "Now that I've had time to get some distance between us, I can see how you controlled me through your anger."

She sucked in her breath. Her eyes glittered. "Time? Since yesterday?" she asked scornfully. "I never tried to control you."

"I can see this is a bad idea. It's just that Anna gave this to me . . . and . . ."

"She *gave* it to you?"

He nodded. "Well, not exactly 'gave' it to me. I inherited it."

"What do you mean?"

"Look, are we going to be adults about this and you let me in, or should I just leave?"

She shrugged and stepped back, opening the door wider. "Come in."

He followed her into the formal living room with its straight-backed chairs and dark end tables on either side of a too-firm sofa. He sat down on it and put the box on the coffee table.

She sat in a side chair and leaned forward, her hand inching towards the box. He put his right hand on the lid.

"Wait. You asked me how I got this. I tried to tell you before, but you always got mad when I talked about Anna."

"I do not like Anna."

He grinned. "So I gathered, but it was important and yet I was too enthralled in your authority over me to defy you."

"What are you talking about!"

"You're an old witch. I mean that," he added hastily, "in terms of years."

She waved his comment by, irritated.

"Raven, you let me know every second we were together that I was a lesser being than you."

Her mouth opened. She started to shake her head, but he held up his hand.

"I wanted to love you, Raven. You never trusted me beyond the bedroom. You never let me talk about anything outside of your own experience. I understand that you've been around a lot longer than I have and seen life in all of its nasty glory, but I got the feeling that you hated me for being innocent and kinda dumb."

"That's ridiculous."

"Is it? Well, we're through, so I can be honest. I'm just telling you that I wanted us to be different. I really loved you for yourself, Raven, not because you could teach me how to cure a boil by using ragweed or mugwort or whatever."

"A poultice of bitter gourd," she said under her breath.

He rolled his eyes. "See? Always the teacher, never my soul mate." He couldn't believe how good it felt not to be on his guard with her and to speak openly and truthfully. He wondered how things might've gone if he'd had the gumption to face her months ago.

She stared down at her hand, still poised over the box and his hand. Slowly, she withdrew it and put it in her lap. "Perhaps you're right. I am sorry you felt me to be so unapproachable. But you are also correct in saying that it doesn't matter anymore."

He nodded. "True. I just want to set the record straight."

"So noted."

"Now." He paused. "This is going to be difficult."

"Get on with it!"

He scooted closer to her. "Anna is dead, Raven."

Her face drained of color. "What? What?"

"I inherited her things because she died. I tried to tell you, but you put that spell on me. I couldn't talk for a week. So I gave up. I know you hated her, but she told me you were close at one time."

"You talked about me? You didn't even know me then!"

"She told me about her life. It was hard, as I expect yours was. Only I wouldn't know, because you never let me into your heart enough to trust me."

"How did she die?" Raven's mouth was tight.

"It was the Spanish flu in 1918."

"Impossible! Witches don't die like that!" Her fists were clenched.

"They do if they are pregnant and trying to save their child's life." Tears came to the corners of his eyes. "It was our child and she was happy. She knew she was dying. The influenza took so many. Over 50 million worldwide. She told me to cut the baby out of her womb. I couldn't, may the moon forgive me. I was scared. I got a doctor. Maybe he was exhausted from helping everyone. Or maybe she was too sick. Or maybe he wasn't a good doctor. I don't know. But she didn't live and the baby died, too."

Raven put her head in her hands. Her chest was heaving, but she was silent. He carefully laid a hand on her shoulder. She leaned slightly into him. He felt his fingertips tingle. So she still was trying to enchant him. It must be part of her nature. Or maybe that meant she still had feelings for him, even unknown to her; otherwise why try to keep the spell going? He tightened his grip on her shoulder, and she squirmed away. *So much for a tender moment.*

When she faced him, her eyes were dry and bright. It was her voice that betrayed her. It was hollow. "She died in agony."

"No," he lied. "The doctor gave her ether."

Squaring her shoulders, she took a deep breath, gathering reserves from deep within. "What's in the box?"

He lifted the lid and took out a black quartz crystal sphere. It was the size of an apricot. Light flickered inside as he rotated it in his palm. She reached for it, her mouth open in awe. This time, he let her take it.

"The Black Moon!" she whispered. "And you kept it in a shoebox!"

He shrugged. "Is it something special, teacher?"

"Don't mock me." She glared at him, then added more softly, "Please."

He raised his eyebrows but she was too busy looking at the orb to see.

"There are only twelve in existence. One for each month of the moon. A thirteenth moon was planned, according to the ancient way of reckoning time, but it broke. Or was destroyed. The legends aren't clear. This is the Black Moon. It disappeared sometime in the century after the Aquarius, or what you call the Christ, was born. It's twenty thousand years old. It was found in a glacier in the Alps."

In spite of himself, Miguel was drawn in. "So, what's it for?"

"It exists in its own right, just as you do."

"Metaphysical emptyspeak!" He tapped the table. "I mean, in practical terms."

Her voice was full of awe. "The Black Moon represents Lilith, Adam's first wife."

"He wasn't married only to Eve? Huh. Well, then, he had already lost his innocence before the apple thing."

"Exactly!" Raven's eyes shone. "Lilith wanted to be Adam's equal, especially sexually. She matched him passion for passion, but he wanted to dominate. So she left him. In the patriarchal stories, she was reviled as a woman from the waist up and a flaming serpent from the waist down." She glared at him. "Men couldn't stand a strong woman, even then."

Miguel threw up his hands. "Whoa! Who are we talking about here? Look, I like a strong woman but I don't want a woman who won't share and wants to be alone all the time."

Surprise flared in her eyes. "You were part of my life!"

He gave an abrupt nod. "That's what I mean. We need to share a life together."

"Need? Past tense, please."

"Yeah. Anyway, I guess Lilith found another husband? Or were all men brutes back then, just like now?"

She ignored his jab. "She never married again. She was alone."

There was a pointed silence. Raven finally cleared her throat. "So," she said, "the Black Moon is a feminine symbol of the darkness that exists, balanced between the sun and the earth. It is a shadow concept. The Black Moon is an unseen reflection of the known."

Miguel mimed pulling his hair out. "Arggh! My brain can't decipher that."

She ignored him and went on. "It is the missing feminine presence represented by the Holy Spirit. Or a woman's need for autonomous identity."

Miguel yawned. "Interesting." Seeing her skeptical look, he rushed to add, "I mean it, but I gotta get back. There're more of Anna's things I need to sort through."

"Anna." The word hung between them like a fist ready to punch her in the gut. He saw her hand shaking, the black ball rocking slightly in her small palm. Something tugged at his heart, but he dismissed it and stood up.

Her voice trembled. She looked up at him with her dark full eyes. She cleared her throat. "Wait. You said there were more items?"

He nodded. "I'll let you know if there's anything interesting."

She started to rise. "Maybe I should look at them myself."

He put his hand out, palm down. "I'll get back to you on that."

He hurried away before he would give in. Someone had to show her who was boss.

"When are you coming back?" she called after him.

Without slowing down or looking back at her, he shrugged. *Trap sprung,* he thought.

4

After the door slammed shut, Raven heard the silence in the house. Emptiness. Again. She sank to the floor and curled up in a ball. Her tears started out quietly, but soon her moans rocked her. The rain drummed down on the roof.

Anna.

Once, Anna and she had been captured by a brutal warlord who kept them captive in a tent. After weeks of beatings and abuse, they were able to escape. Anna stole a horse and rode off, while Raven was forced to jump into the river to avoid a man with a battle-ax. They'd promised to meet at the Pillars of Hercules as soon as they could.

It was over two years before she saw Anna again, although she had waited for her at the Pillars for weeks. And when she did see Anna, her friend was laughing on the arm of a handsome young man.

It was in a market in southern Iberia, not far from the Pillars, that rocky outcropping known today as Gibraltar.

Anna waved gaily at Raven and smiled. "There you are!"

Raven stood shocked. "We were supposed to meet! Years ago! Do you know what I went through to get here?"

Anna snuggled closer to the man, who looked bored. The women were talking in an old language he didn't understand.

"Oh, I knew you were all right. I did a location spell on you and knew you were fine." She bent closer. "I had to stay with Aerlik. He's got the most magnificent carriage and a huge house. I'm his First Teacher, so we are having a delicious time." Anna tilted her head. "Don't look at me like that. You made it safely and so did I. Life goes on, doesn't it?"

Raven stared wordlessly as her friend sauntered off.

It was not the last time that Anna would let Raven down. And now she was gone, dead for almost a century, and Raven had had no sense of the leaving, no ripping of the magic fabric of the universe. She shuddered. How could life change so utterly in one day? Yesterday, she'd thought Anna was alive, her enemy and sister, and the world had been understood. It had been she and Anna dancing around the pole of life, weaving friendship and hatred, spells and adventures. Now, she was really alone. There was no shadow sister, no Black Moon in her life.

She gazed into the crystal Moon, dark as soot. What could it reveal to her? She shook it gently. Nothing stirred. She knew her powers were waning. She was getting very old. Crow's-feet were etched into the corners of her eyes. And her jowls were sagging slightly. It was another reason to be alone. She couldn't expect Miguel to love her as she slowly aged, becoming more mortal and less incandescent. No, it was right to banish him from her heart. Uneasy, she turned away from her thoughts.

Two days later, Miguel sat outside her house in his car. He'd deliberately avoided calling her or stopping by. He wanted to whet her curiosity. He wanted her to be eager to see him and any of Anna's treasures.

The problem was that he didn't really have much more to give her. On the seat next to him he had a piece of yellowed lace and a tattered strip of ivory ribbon. It had been carefully pressed between two layers of tissue paper and laid inside a wooden box. The box was cherry wood polished to a mirror-bright sheen. He snapped the lid closed and picked it up. Getting out of the car, he walked to her door.

He rang the bell, running his spiel through his head. He had to get her attention. He had to flirt with her. She had to want him again.

He cleared his throat. He was nervous.

But no one answered the door. He was achingly disappointed.

5

He came back the next morning. The box, about fist size, was in one hand. The other hand twitched anxiously in his pocket, jingling some coins. He took a deep breath and forced himself to calm down. Jeez, what was this? He was in control, perfect control.

Wasn't he?

The door opened so abruptly that he was caught off guard. Any rehearsed speech went out of his brain. She wore a long black dress with tight-fitting sleeves that flared out over her delicate wrists. A large, milky stone dangled from a silver chain by her collarbone. He stammered hello, struck again by the effect she had on him. What kind of spell was she using, anyway?

"Uh."

"'Uh' to you, too," she said wryly.

He scuffed his feet. "I found this." He held out the box.

"Come in," she said. He looked great. Black tee and jeans. Leather bracelets with tiny turquoise bird fetishes worked in among the knots. Quickly she told herself to forget about that. She stepped back for him to enter. This time she led him to her study, their shoes tapping across the walnut flooring. She gestured to a leather easy chair. He folded himself into it. She chose a matching chair next to an ebony side table.

Seated, she took the box from him and lifted the lid.

"I found it with some of Anna's stuff," he explained. "Maybe it might hold some memories?"

She took out the lace and ribbon, smoothing them carefully on her lap. She shook her head. "No, I don't know about this, but I'm picking up vibes. She wore it in . . . the early 1700s. She was living as a noblewoman in France. Hmm. It was from a dress. Her wedding dress." She looked up at him. "That's all I see."

He shrugged. "Well, I guess that's it. Sorry." He put his hands on his knees, preparing to get up.

She'd started to put the lace back in the box when she froze. "Wait a minute. I am getting more from the box!" She closed her eyes.

He watched her. She was lovely. He shook himself and eased back down.

"Ah." A smile tugged at her lips. She opened her eyes. "It's not the box per se, but the wood itself. Cherry wood is symbolic of death, rebirth, and awakenings. Also love." She glanced at his eyes and then quickly looked down. "This box is old. It was part of a cradle. A baby boy." She smiled softly. "The tree grew in a garden of a woman who prayed for years to have that baby. When the boy was born, the tree was struck by lightning, so her husband made the cradle from its wood.

"The tree called itself Everwood. When the lightning struck its heart, it knew it was dying. But there is still memory in its cells, and I feel its happiness to have been made into a cradle. Years later, the cradle burned in a house fire, and all that was salvaged was wood enough to make this box. The boy grew up and gave it to his wife. She kept his love letters in it when he went to war. He returned home safely." She stroked the lid. "Thank you for bringing this, Miguel. It's very special and I am sure Anna treasured it. You see, it imparts the holder with peace and joy."

He frowned. "I didn't feel anything." He was a little embarrassed to admit it.

"Well, that happens. Some objects connect more with certain people." She shrugged. "I do not know why."

He fidgeted. "I . . . I suppose I should go."

"But, Miguel, I thought you were coming over to pick up your things earlier this week. In fact, I waited quite awhile." She was annoyed.

"Zorro was busy, but, uh, I promise we'll come over tomorrow. Are you in a rush?"

"No. I suppose not." She shrugged again. "It's just that I was expecting you, and, really, you could've called to say you'd been delayed."

He hadn't called because he was trying to make a point. But now he could see that he'd merely been rude. "I'm sorry." He bit his lip. "I'll call you before I come tomorrow to confirm. Is that OK?"

She nodded and stood up. She handed the box back to him, but he pushed it away.

"No, Raven. It's yours. Keep it."

"Thank you." She put the box down on the end table. She hesitated. "Would you like some cold water? Or tea?"

"Uh." He was struck by wanting to stay and feeling he should keep her off balance and go. He cleared his throat. "I should get back. Still trying to clean up my junk."

"Fine." She started walking to the door.

"But," he said suddenly, "maybe a glass of water would hit the spot."

"Of course."

"I can get it myself," he said.

"No, it's my house," she said coolly. "You're my guest." She exited and he followed her. She glanced back and stopped, raising an eyebrow.

"I'll just come along with you, is that OK?" At her nod, he followed, feeling like a big, clumsy puppy.

24

In the kitchen, she went to the cupboard and grabbed a glass. Meanwhile, he'd turned on the faucet, letting the water run cold.

"Ice?" she asked.

"You know I don't like ice," he said, surprised.

She shrugged and handed him the glass. "Who knows? Perhaps you've changed in the last few days."

He filled the glass, trying to contain his anger. But he couldn't help himself. He whirled around. "I'm not the one who changed. You stopped loving me. I didn't stop loving you."

As soon as he said it, his cheeks flamed.

She gave him a stony look. "I suppose you're right. I did stop loving you."

His face paled. He felt sick to his stomach, and the glass shook in his hand. He set it down carefully on the counter. The ugly words felt like a stab in the heart.

"So," she continued, "you must stop trying to get me back using that bungled charm. It's so weak and trembling. I don't know where you learned it, but it's comical. You should be humiliated."

His mouth dropped open. "I'm not . . . not using any spells!"

Her mouth twitched. "Of course you are."

"No, I am not," he said emphatically. "Which is more than I can say for you! Talk about calling the witch black . . ."

"Me!" Her head reared back. "I am not enchanting you! Why would I?"

"Oh, yeah?" He was aware he sounded like a sixth-grader. "Oh, yeah? Then why do I feel sparks when I touch you? Look." He reached out to her shoulder. She tried to step back but the counter blocked her retreat. As soon as he touched her, a jolt hit them both.

They gasped.

She recovered quickly. "It's only static electricity."

"Right." His voice dipped. "You're always right." He stepped back. "The humidity must be 110 percent. How could there be static?"

She shrugged. "I don't know but does it matter? To me, it does not." She moved away, stepping around him, and heading toward the door. He had no choice but to follow her.

"Call me when you're on your way tomorrow," she said, holding the door for him.

He nodded. On the porch, he turned around. "I . . ." But he was speaking to a closed door. He stared at it for a moment, shocked and . . . angry.

25

6

"So, what did you expect?" Zorro shoved a beer toward Miguel. They were sitting outside on the patio. It was sunny and all of Seattle basked in the bright rays.

Miguel popped the tab and chugged a big gulp. He didn't bother answering.

Zorro grabbed a handful of salted macadamia nuts. He spoke around a mouthful. "I knew this would happen." He swallowed. "It never was about you showing her who was boss. Uh-uh. You didn't want to be dumped cuz you're still into her. Big-time. She's got you by the short hairs, amigo."

"Shut up." Miguel slumped down in the chair.

Zorro ignored him. "The way I see it, you got two choices. One, you can really give her up. Or two, you can go after her, woo her all over again."

Miguel grimaced. "I did give her up, Z. You're reading this all wrong."

"Sure I am."

Miguel rolled his eyes. "How about if we talk about you for a change. Like, what are you studying now, besides meddling in my business?"

"Glad you asked. Cuz my business is your biz, brother."

"Jeez." Miguel had to laugh. "Z, you're something else."

Zorro grinned. "C'mon. Let's lay your cards on the table. Bare your soul. Tell me the truth."

Miguel sighed and started talking. It was the only way to shut Z up.

Raven paced her study. Bookshelves lined three walls. The fourth wall was a large pane of glass. Outside, her garden was bathed in bright sunshine. Flowers crowded one another in an old-fashioned cottage garden; paving stones were set haphazardly in a winding path. But she hardly noticed the view. Chewing on a fingernail, she wondered if she was losing her mind as well as her ability to cast spells.

She could've sworn he was using a come-hither spell. But now that she thought of it, she hadn't sensed any personal spells around him for ages. Once, she had called him on a teeth-whitening spell, teasing him about his teeth lighting up the night. She tapped the nail against her own front tooth. Had she ever sensed any kind of love charm around him?

No, she mused. She had not. In the beginning, he'd been so gaga over her she had felt only his charming attraction. A powerful, but completely natural, pull. Of course, she told herself calmly, she had never been *that* in love with him. He had been a pleasant diversion, a nice tumble in bed, but nothing permanent. Never that.

So, why, she asked herself, *why the hell am I so . . . lonely?*

"Without him," she whispered, completing the thought.

This won't do.

She stood still. Thoughts raced through her mind. *I don't need a man, especially not him. I am fine by myself. I have always managed alone. He's too young.*

Or I have lived too long.

She sighed. Her hands clenched. She looked around the room. Like others before it, it reflected her love of studying. Books that belonged in museums, artifacts that pulsated with power, and bowls of crystals—everything on the shelves had traveled with her from one home to the other through the ages. She had lost much, of course, in hasty escapes in the middle of the night, one step ahead of village mobs. Crates of her possessions had sunk into the sea, been stolen, or simply disappeared.

Perhaps it was time to move again. She groaned. She liked it here. However, it would be for the best. To leave. To avoid . . . what? She shook her head, forcing herself to admit the truth.

She needed to avoid Miguel. To avoid loving him. To avoid, ultimately, losing him.

"What a fragile soul you are," she said, disgusted.

She went over to her casting table and lifted the shoebox lid. Inside, on a bed of cotton padding, gleamed the Black Moon orb. She picked it up and went over to her desk by the window. Sitting down, she placed it on the desk and stared at it.

Surely, she should be able to see her future in its dark mists. *Tell me what to do,* she demanded. Nothing happened. The globe was opaque. Frustrated, she shook it and turned it over. Still nothing. What did she expect? It wasn't a Magic 8 Ball, predicting *yes, no, maybe, ask again later.* She put it down.

But maybe in its darkness was the answer. *I'm not Lilith,* she thought, *running away from a domineering man. Miguel never tried to take over my life. I made sure of that by parceling out my moments with him. I never gave all of myself,* she admitted. *So why am I running away? Or, more precisely, who am I running from?*

All the centuries of leaving, vanishing, escaping. Her children, all dead but one, and who knew about that one? The last she'd heard, Gazera had been in India, but that was fifty—no, seventy—years ago. The older she got, the more she lost.

As she looked one last time into the Black Moon's depths, it came to her in a flash. It wasn't Love or Miguel that she was running away from.

It was Death.

7

Miguel and Zorro lifted the crated sixty-four-inch plasma TV carefully and angled it through the doorway. They grunted directions to each other as Miguel walked backward. Raven stepped out of the way. He loved that contraption, spending hours watching sports and cooking shows while she pored through old texts and unfolded codices.

Zorro nodded at her as he passed. Their voices echoed along the hallway. She followed them out to the truck. They loaded up, bracing the huge crate with several boxes. Miguel jumped down from the bed. Zorro leaned against the fender and wiped his forehead with the back of his hand.

"That's about it," Miguel said.

She nodded, biting her lip. There was a lump in her throat. It seemed final. He was out of her life.

Zorro said, "Sure could use a beer about now."

"I don't have beer." She didn't like alcohol.

"Sí, I forgot." Zorro sighed. "Well, something cold?"

"I have water."

"Guess that will have to do."

"Let's sit in the patio here," she directed, pointing to a small table and four chairs by the fountain. The courtyard was bordered by tall hedges for privacy, and the patio was decorated with tubs of blooming roses and pink petunias. Both of the men took a seat while Raven disappeared into the house. She returned a few minutes later, carrying a tray with three glasses and some napkins.

"Here we go." She handed out the glasses and set the tray down by her side on the bricks.

They sipped quietly.

Zorro's nose twitched. These *novios* needed a nudge, but what could he do? All he had was his affinity to air. And that's when he got an idea. He started whistling, a soft tune that sounded like two mating birds calling to each other. Raven looked over at him curiously. He put on an innocent face. "Hey, Miguel, tell her what we're gonna do." He whistled again.

Miguel shifted in his seat. "Well, Z and I are thinking . . ."

Suddenly, on the last note of Zorro's tune, wind blew up, swirling across the patio, knocking over the water glasses and picking up pieces of grit and dirt. Miguel jumped up to grab a glass at the same time that Raven did. With an audible clunk, they bumped heads.

Miguel rocked backward and swore. Raven teetered on her heels before sinking into her seat, hand to her forehead.

"Oh!" She let out a gasp. She was seeing stars and black moons and spinning red hearts.

Zorro stood up, gathering the glasses in one big hand. The wind died down. Water dripped over the edge of the table, soaking the paper napkins.

"I'll get a towel," Zorro said as he quickly went into the house. A glance back showed him that Miguel was bending over Raven, asking her if she was okay. Zorro grinned. His spell worked pretty good. All the elements were there: Raven and fire, Miguel and water, himself as air, and the swirling bits of sand represented earth. He was feeling proud of himself as he put the dirty glasses in the sink, tucked some paper towels under his arm, and filled three new glasses with fresh water. He spied a package of cookies on the counter, and, holding it between his teeth, he managed to carry everything out to the patio.

Miguel had drawn his chair closer to Raven. She was laughing a little and holding her forehead with one hand.

Zorro mumbled. Miguel rose and took the package of cookies from his mouth. Zorro said, "Hope you don't mind I got these cookies. I'm a bit hungry. Miguel, can you grab the towels and wipe the mess up?"

Soon everything was sorted out, and they sat down again.

"Now, as I was saying before that little wind blew up," said Zorro, "Miguel and I have made new plans. Did you tell her yet?"

Raven eyed Zorro. Did he have something to do with the sudden gust? But Miguel was speaking.

"No. I didn't say anything yet." Miguel looked uneasy.

"What?" asked Raven.

"Z and I are thinking of moving."

"I also am thinking of that," she said.

Miguel stared at her. "You are?"

She nodded. "Where are you going?"

Miguel was silent. Zorro spoke up. "South, maybe back to Mexico. My spells don't work right up here. It's all that damp. You need an oil can just to charm a wart off," he joked.

Raven pursed her lips. "I don't know, Z. Your spells seem to work quite well." She looked at him pointedly, but he just gave her a small smile.

"Actually," she added, "I am returning to Mexico. I am thinking San Carlos or maybe Puerto Vallarta. One can live quite well there, and the climate is pleasant."

Miguel put a shaky hand on her shoulder. "What would you think if we tagged along?"

She took his hand off her shoulder, and his face fell. But then she placed his hand between her two hands and squeezed. "I think that would be an excellent idea, boys." She smiled at Miguel, who scooted closer.

Zorro stood up quietly and went out to stand by his truck. He waited until he heard her door close. Miguel didn't come out, so after a few more moments of waiting, Zorro got in the truck. "You sly old fox," he grinned at himself. Life isn't about fear; it's about love. *I should write a song,* he thought, as he shoved the key in and drove back home, bouncing on the seat and singing, "Ay, Ay, Ay!"

WHITE BUTTERFLIES

NEAR THE RIO YAQUI, SONORA, MEXICO, 1530s

Mother carried Kuta in from her work in the fields, her breath rasping in fear. He had the spotted sickness.

We wrapped him in soft rabbit fur to encourage sweating, then bathed him in cool water. I had a small packet of scraped *wata,* river willow bark. I made a tea of it and dribbled it into his mouth. He quieted for a while, his eyes closed softly. I sat back on my heels, so frightened I could barely swallow. I was relieved that he slept peacefully, though.

It was only a short time later when he woke up screaming. The high-pitched wails pierced my ears. His sores burst open, pus streaking the sleeping mat under his flushed body. We wiped him down.

Mother had a headache and lay back on her mat with a cool cloth over her eyes. She said it felt like cactus needles inserted under her eyelids.

Kuta farted bloody mucus. I cleaned him with fresh water. Hurrying outside, I rooted in our storage platforms, built from cane high off the ground so that the rats wouldn't eat our food. There were some old maize ears covered with smut, a darkish fungus. I scraped some off and climbed back down the ladder. Dropping a pinch of the smut into a drinking gourd, I stirred it with my finger. He wouldn't want to drink it, but it would help his diarrhea.

Using a thin bamboo straw, I poured it into him, then followed it with some mesquite tea, which was good for a fever. Finally, his eyes closed again. While he slept, I looked at Mother. She had spots.

Grandmother, who had been visiting one of her friends, came home late that afternoon. She collapsed in front of the house near the loom. I pulled her in, my arms shaking, and gave her the mesquite tea. Grey half-circles shadowed the skin under her eyes. Angry red spots bloomed on her cheeks.

30

Rubbing my eyes tiredly, I looked around. The sun filtered through the woven cane walls, striking the sleeping figures with long spears of light. A water gourd lay overturned, forgotten. The air was tainted with the sour smells of vomit, pus, and feverish bodies. In the dim corners, death seemed to wait, coiled like a snake.

Suddenly, Kuta convulsed. He arched his back, whining, legs thrashing as he banged his head on the ground. I held him firmly, frightened at how rigid his body was. Abruptly he went limp. I didn't know what to do, so I cried. Everyone was sick and I was too young. I didn't know enough. I tried to heal them with my hands, but my blood felt like corn popping in the fire.

Kuta died as the third day dawned. I wrapped him in the soiled rabbit fur and laid his body outside.

Mother scratched her sores, moaning as her fingers tore bloody gashes in her flesh. She was delirious. I tried to tie her arms down, but she flailed, striking me in the nose. I cried again as the blood trickled down my chin.

Pus sealed her eyes shut. Her tongue was so swollen that she couldn't close her mouth; yellow pus seeped into her throat or flowed over her chin, where it dried in thick, crusty streaks.

I washed her with warm water, gently easing the torn and diseased skin. Patches of her back stuck to the mat in a bloody mess. Dabbing jojoba juice on her wounds took a long time. I was careful but still she shrieked in pain.

Grandmother never woke up. She had fewer sores but the fever burnt out her soul. I rolled her body, so light and brittle, into the sleeping mat and tugged it outside next to Kuta.

I was so tired. I gulped gourds of mesquite tea. My skin itched. I had five spots. My head felt like a water drum. A pounding headache sent me reeling. I could see my mother plucking the air with shriveled fingers.

"Ai, Mother. What are you doing?" I asked her.

I leaned close to her cracked lips. "They come. They come to me."

"Who?"

"Butterflies."

We believed that white butterflies took our souls away to the western land of the dead. I shuddered. Shivering, I crawled into bed with her.

"No! Mother, please don't die!" I held her hand, then curled up next to her. If I was going to die, I didn't want to die alone.

I lay on the mat, crying for Kuta. Dead! I would never see his eyes twinkling at me again. My name was silenced forever on his tongue.

And my grandmother. She was gone up to the stars, joining our ancestors.

Where was my father?

There was a heavy stillness. It was either twilight or dawn or someplace between time and breath. An opaque light seeped into the house, obscuring the familiar shapes, twisting the dried chilies hanging from the rafter into masses of dark red scorpions, changing the bunches of wild sage into hanks of witchy hair, transforming baskets into piles of split heads. I groaned, turning my head slowly, toward the sounds of footsteps.

In the doorway, a dark shape wavered as I squinted.

"Father?" I whispered.

The shape came closer and knelt. It was Seahamut. She stroked my hot forehead, murmuring. She poured a little water into my mouth, wiping my chin with her long hair. Bare-breasted, she wore only a shell necklace and a rustling grass skirt. She looked young, cheeks curving firmly, eyes sparkling even as I sensed her sadness. It was hard to keep my eyes open. I was glad she was here to help. I sighed, feeling her calm strength as she tended to my mother and made more medication.

Then she came to my side again. "Sleep. You won't die. Your mother rests and does not need you. Sleep."

Feebly, I protested. "Kuta . . ."

"All will be taken care of," she promised. Her black hair enveloped her in a cloud. I couldn't see her very well. I rubbed my eyes. Was I speaking to a shadow? Or was I going blind?

Her shape dimmed as I fell into a restless sleep.

Mother could see only dark and light. She mumbled when she spoke, making no sense at first, but I could see that Seahamut was right. We both would live. Every day, I bathed Mother, cleaning away rotted skin; the scabs fell off when I rubbed gently. I treated her with ointments to prevent infection.

My mother no longer sang. Her voice was harsh, if she spoke at all. I fed her maize gruel. We had been sick for many days, but we had plenty of food. Peppers. Chilies. Beans. Ground maize. Dried fish and deer meat.

But I was not hungry. My feet traveled on their own, far from my head. I would arrive at the drying rack, wondering why I had walked there. I poured water over my thumb when I meant to take a drink. My thoughts rattled around like two stones in an empty gourd.

I couldn't find my grandmother's body. Or Kuta's. I saw plenty of coyote tracks by our door but no bodies. Maybe the coyotes took the bodies. But how? There were no drag marks, no blood. I was confused. Then I remembered Seahamut. Hadn't she told me she would take care of everything? At first I thought her visit was only a fever dream, but it seemed she'd actually been in the house.

One morning when I was feeling stronger, I went to look for my father. I had a few deep scars on my stomach, and my skin was sloughing off in ragged bits. As I shed my ravaged skin, my new skin grew paler than before. My nose was raw and I limped. But I was alive.

I took several deep breaths, considering where I should look for my father. He loved fishing, so I would go to the sea. He might still be sick and needing me.

Birds sang. It was the time of the year when the desert cools down. The air was clear, every rock and twig sharply defined. I walked on shaky legs.

The river estuary was marshy and contained somewhat by the shifting sand dunes. The trails that wound between the largest dunes were never the same from year to year. The sand slithered under my feet so that it took ten steps where one should've sufficed. Finally, I sat down, exhausted. It was not so far, really, I told myself. My right leg trembled.

I laid my head against the sand. *Why am I here?* I had to remind myself that I must find my father. I was so tired. Nothing seemed more important than the warm sand beneath me, shifting to support the contours of my body. As my eyes drooped, I saw a small lizard with Kuta's eyes staring at me before it dashed away.

I sat up. The marsh grass flashed gray and green as the wind twisted it into waves. A brown pelican flew overhead, the air instantly filled with the heavy flapping of its immense wings. Stiffly, I got to my feet.

How could life change so quickly? A short time ago my mother had been grinding maize, slapping tortillas on the *copal,* and singing. Now she was half blind. I'd seen her cradling her arms as if Kuta was still sleeping there. She rocked and hummed, sometimes nodding her head and smiling.

Kuta had been fun to watch as he waved his toes and fingers in the air like an upturned beetle. He'd practice forming bubbles on his lips. I'd pop them with my finger while he chuckled.

Grandmother had a good sense of humor, too. For example, she had a beautiful tattoo of a fish on her upper arm. One day it was gone.

"Where's your fish?" I asked.

"I ate it, I was so hungry last night." She smiled, winking.

I puzzled over that for days until she took pity on me and showed me what happened. To make the tattoo, she'd taken the spine of a mesquite tree. After poking a design onto her arm, she'd crushed the leaves of the same tree into the holes. A lovely green-blue color patterned her skin.

"But," she said, "when you get tired of it, all you do is to prick those same holes again. The dye will come out with a little blood. The tattoo will disappear."

For a split second, I had believed she'd eaten the fish, but I was too embarrassed to admit it. I liked the joke, even if it was at my own expense. I decided to jest, myself.

"No, I thought it jumped off your arm and back into the river!"

She laughed a long time over that, then hurried off to tell Mother. Soon, I could hear them both giggling. I got angry. I thought they were laughing at me. I felt stupid. They didn't understand I was teasing. They thought I was still a baby. I ran off into the desert, where I sat with a scowl on my face, brooding.

Now, if only Grandmother were here again, I could put my arms around her and tickle her chin. I wanted to hear that deep belly laugh of hers. Who will tell me about the old days? Who will tickle me awake every morning? My chest was tight with the thought that I'd never see her again, weaving at the loom, or singing sleeping songs to Kuta.

I had to find my father. He would help Mother. I wouldn't be so alone. He'd watch over us.

I could hear the waves pounding the shore on the other side of the sand dunes. Rounding the last bend in the trail, I stopped to view the ocean.

My father loved the sea, unlike many other of the People, who preferred the mountains or the desert.

He took me out once in his cane boat, but I got sick.

I looked for the boat. It was made of bamboo lashed together. But I didn't see anything on the beach. I strode down to the wet sand, where walking was easier.

Father fished alone. I guess he liked the solitude. I understood that. Knowing how I liked the desert solitude, he once told me that the ocean was like a "wet desert."

The long beach was littered with shells both broken and whole, tattered crab shells left from marauding seabirds, and seaweeds with bladder pods. I stepped carefully, not wanting to cut my bare feet. The tide was low. The sea was a distant deep blue. White waves rolled in, while the sand sucked at my feet. Tiny holes opened in the sand as the water retreated from each wave.

The sun was hot but I didn't stop searching.

My father was here somewhere. It was one of his favorite fishing spots. He told me we Yoemem used to fish the oceans in canoes large enough for ten men. There was one such canoe beached not far from the river's mouth. It was half buried in river silt. Father pointed it out to me long ago.

"This was made by my grandfather's grandfather. Or his grandfather. It was a good war canoe."

"It's so big!" I remarked.

"It was cut in the mountains and then floated down the river. There used to be big trees when the land was wetter." He explained how it was hollowed out with fire and ax. He was disgusted that it lay rotting. Few were interested in doing things the old way, he said. Then, true to his nature, he laughed.

"My father said the same thing about the youth of his day!"

My father was never serious very long. That's why my mother loved him. She said it made life easier when you laughed.

I didn't think I'd ever laugh again.

The wind blew from the sea. It was a small sea, according to my father.

"On the other side of the waters are cliffs and mountains."

"Is it a big land?"

"No, it looks like this." He took my hand and separated my thumb from my fingers. "The other land looks like your thumb."

I wiggled it.

"If you follow your thumb up," he continued, "you would come to more land, a big place, like your hand. Where the thumb meets the fingers, here. Yes, this fleshy part. There's a river there that has red water, and it spills into our sea. More people live there but they aren't as good as us."

I nodded. Of course! No one was better than the People!

"Yet it's been said that we came from the land near this river long ago," he added.

"I thought we came from the Flower World."

Scratching his ear, he paused to think. "Well, we have a spiritual birthplace, beyond myth and memory. A place where souls live. That is one way of thinking."

"Ummm." I was confused.

"Or perhaps the Flower World is a memory of a real place full of flowers and rivers. But we haven't seen it for so long that we don't know if it's real or not."

"Why don't we just go there?" I was ready to set off at once.

"The land changes, Chikul. I have seen stone fish in the mountains. Some say it's magic, but I wonder if the fish lived there once."

"What! Fish in the mountains! And how could fish become stones?"

He laughed at my questions. "Perhaps the mountains were at the bottom of the sea long ago."

"No!" I scrunched up my face. This wasn't possible.

He shrugged. "I admit I don't know. But I've thought about this a lot while I'm fishing." He motioned for us to sit. When his arm was around me, he continued. "Maybe our original homeland was a place in time, rather than a location."

I didn't understand.

"A time, Chikul, when the rains fell more often and flowers covered the earth." He looked up at the sky. "Some say we have always been here. Maybe they're right. It was wetter once and the desert bloomed. *This* is where the

Flower World was." He nodded to himself, then pointed to his chest. "And *here* is where it still is."

I never wanted to leave this land. It was everything to me. Here all my relatives lived.

Or had lived until this terrible sickness. Who was still alive? Was it only our house that had such sickness?

I shaded my eyes. Not too far away, there was a clump of sea plants and scraps of cloth. I ran toward it.

At first my eye couldn't take in the parts. I saw the whole, a jumble of seaweed, driftwood, gull feathers . . . and something else.

I peered closer. It smelled awful. As I identified part of a bloated hand, I put my fist in my mouth. There were broken bamboo and strips of faded red cloth. A finger, chewed to the bone, floated in a sea puddle. Small black crabs crawled over the flesh. Was this part of my father? How could I know?

With a stick I poked, pulling aside seaweed and mounds of sand. A man's arm emerged. Where was the rest of the body?

I walked some distance away and sat down to think. If my father had been sick on the boat, he may have drifted for days. I couldn't remember what clothes he'd been wearing when he left.

The flesh was blackened from days in the sun, and putrid. I'd seen signs of sores on the arm. The pustules were broken and clean, the pus having been washed away. This could be my father, but there were other fishermen, of course, and the boat could've drifted from any place. This could even be a Seri, those people who lived north of us.

Without warning, the tears came. My father must be dead. I sobbed until my throat was raw. I hadn't thought I'd ever cry again after all that I'd been through, but my grief was terrible. My father was dead, I told myself again. He'd never leave us this long unless he was.

Maybe now, I thought, *he knows where the Flower World is.*

From the corner of my eye, I noticed a movement and turned quickly. It was a vulture, waiting for me to leave. I screamed at it, but it only rustled its dark feathers, and settled back down on the dune, eyeing the remains on the sand.

WHERE THE BONES ARE

SONORA, MEXICO, 1530S

I smelled smoke. I started running home, sliding on the sand, fear engulfing me. Smoke billowed up near my home.

Had the cooking fire flared up? Was she in danger? I should've never left her alone.

I skidded to a stop as I passed the fence of mesquite and cacti that surrounded our home. Mother stood, slightly bent, with a thin cotton shawl wrapped around her shoulders. Her unbrushed hair was covered with falling ash.

"Mother! *Ae!*"

She turned toward the sound of my voice. "Burn. Burn."

Our house was smoldering. The palm mat roof had caved in, the support poles were black and smoking, the interior was a charred mess of broken pots. Everything was ruined. I was speechless.

"Burn. Sickness." Mother tried to explain. She pulled off the shawl and her clothes and threw them into the flames, motioning for me to do the same.

Now we were naked. I saw the *comal,* or flat cooking stone, the pestle and mortar, and field tools propped against a tree. The granary had been spared. She had stored some simple cotton ponchos in a bamboo chest on the platform. I got them and we threw them over our bodies.

Our People's houses had been swept away by floods and shredded by fierce winds in the past. But we'd all been together then. It was easy to rebuild. We *wanted* to rebuild. Now we were few and weak and discouraged. I plopped down on the ground.

My mother sat on her gaunt haunches next to me. Our faces were streaked with soot. She sobbed and threw warm ashes on her legs, gulping and howling until I covered my ears. I remembered a story Father once told me.

There was *Wo'i,* Coyote, who was hunting one day. He found a stinkbug, *juva chinai,* and was going to eat it, when the bug swore that it knew the secrets of the Enchanted World.

"I can tell you what the spirits are saying," it promised.

Coyote took his paw off the bug and cocked an ear. "What are they saying, then?"

The stinkbug listened. "The Spirit People say that any dirty Wo'i who leaves his shit lying around for other animals to step on will burn in a big fire."

Coyote gasped. He raced along the desert, picking up his dung, as well as other animals' droppings. The stinkbug giggled and took off in the other direction.

Like Coyote, I wanted to hurry away from this place of burning. The shit of death. The reeking bed mats. The fever. The house fire. The destruction of all that was important to me. I wanted to run into the desert and never come back. But I didn't want to be foolish like Wo'i. I had responsibilities.

I grabbed baskets of food and tied them around my waist. The living fence of mesquite and prickly pear would soon crowd out the remains of the house. The loom would blow over in the first big winds. The granary platform would topple to the earth.

It was time to leave.

Like a child, Mother held on to my hand. I gave her a walking cane, and she shuffled her way to the river.

"Let's wash ourselves, Mother," I suggested, kneeling on the sand. The river trickled by, from mountain to the sea, not caring that it was washing away our grief.

We made grass skirts, drank our fill, and slept. Then we made our way to the field shelter. In the middle of the maize fields, Father had built a lean-to, a place to nap or get out of the hot sun.

We stayed there. During the day, I searched for other survivors. My uncle's home stank of death. I called and called. But no one answered. I ran away. The neighbors across the river were dead, flies swarming over the rotted flesh and bones.

I went to Seahamut's house. It was built in the traditional way with a roof of woven sticks and palm. The walls, loosely intertwined bamboo, let in the breeze. Three rooms opened on two sides connected by doorways. There was the sleeping room, the workroom, and the storage area. Seahamut's storeroom contained drying herbs and plaited yucca baskets full of roots and packets of prepared medications. Everything had been neat and orderly. I had spent many happy hours there, following Seahamut's directions: cutting, mixing, pounding, steeping, and measuring herbal medications.

It was an awful shock to see it again. The house was burned down. I saw a scorched skull and small gnawed bones. I knew it was Seahamut.

In a daze, I trudged back through the desert and then into our fields. The cultivated land was a narrow strip, close to the river, bordered by the desert.

When I reached the lean-to, I had another surprise. There was a young woman talking to my mother.

Her name was White Star, *Tosali Choki*. She told us that some of the People survived.

"But many of the strong men are dead. And the young mothers. The babies and the old." She looked at us. "You're very lucky to be alive."

The spotted disease maimed as well as killed people. Many were left with scarred faces. One girl had lost part of her lips due to the deep sores. Others were blinded or left feeble-minded, following the healthier with leashes around their wrists. White Star's face was pitted. I tried not to stare and wondered, suddenly, what I looked like.

"Come to Potam with me." Potam was a village not too far away. White Star held my mother's hand and stroked it gently. I wanted to go, but Mother shook her head.

White Star looked around. "You can't stay here. This is not a home. It's a temporary camp. Come to Potam and we can all be together. That's what we are, a People."

"No. No. No." Mother beat her heels on the ground. I'd told her how I'd found remains I thought were Father, but she didn't believe me. I knew she wanted to stay in case he came back.

"We'll stay here," I said, sadly. White Star was sympathetic.

"If she changes her mind, you can come and stay with me. It's not far." She got up from the dirt floor and beckoned to me. I followed her out to the edge of the fields.

"Sometimes the older ones are like this," she said, gesturing back toward my mother. "It's hard for them to see the changes, but we must go on. Give her some time."

"She's like a child now. I think her mind was affected."

White Star nodded. "It's been a terrible time. She's lost a lot. Her mind dwells on the losses, but soon she should see that she has her life and she has you."

She told me that some of the healthy men were going around and burning the contaminated dwellings. Now I knew what had happened to Seahamut's house. White Star explained that at the next full moon, all of the People will meet in Vikam to see who was still living. If Mother wouldn't move to Potam, I'd take her to Vikam, at least, for the meeting.

White Star hugged me and made me promise to visit her. I watched her walk away and wished I was with her. I was angry at my mother. I kicked the dirt. The maize fields needed water, but I hadn't opened the irrigation gates. I didn't care much.

Then I thought how upset my father would've been to see the parched plants and how proud he was of his work. I hurried to the ditches and set to work. I lifted the planks that dammed the channels. Soon water was flowing. I walked to the river, checking for debris that could clog the ditches.

On the riverbank I had my third surprise of the day. A small white puppy lay panting in the shade of the willows. She had a tuft of hair between her ears. Otherwise she was hairless. Southern traders brought her kind to our land, along with parrots and other coveted goods. Many people ate these dogs, but I didn't like dog meat.

The puppy jumped up and ran to me. Her ears lowered to her neck in a sign of delight, she squirmed while she nuzzled my toes. I picked her up, smiling. She was very warm. I dug into my bag for a bit of dried meat and fed it to her. Delicately, she ate it and licked my face. I laughed so hard I had to sit down. We played together. I decided to call her *Paaros,* Jack Rabbit, because she had long ears.

I watched her tail wagging. I made plans to sew a small rabbit cape for her during the winter, and then later when the hot season came again, I'd make a grass cape. I'd tie it around her neck and take care of her. Maybe now things would go right. I had a feeling that life was getting better.

"What is this?" Mother raised her eyebrows when I returned home, carrying Paaros. I blinked. Mother seemed to be more alert, even curious. I told her how I'd found my new dog.

She leaned closer to me and touched my cheek. "It's been so hard for you. I've been thinking ever since White Star came. She's right. We should go to Potam. But, Chikul, can we wait a little longer?"

"Of course!" I smiled. My mother was coming back to her senses.

"You've been so brave, so good, daughter." She kissed my nose. "I've been lost for a long time. Everything was gray. Your voice sounded so far away. I've been living in the shadows."

Paaros wiggled free from my arms and climbed into my mother's lap. She stroked the dog.

"Chikul, when I saw White Star this afternoon, I suddenly remembered I was living. The colors came back. I saw your sadness. Children should be happy."

"I'm almost a woman, Mother." I would be twelve this season. We were through with the time of the deep desert heat. The days were slowing; winter was coming. It was the season when the air would chill at night and storms would boil up over the sea.

"Aiii. Time goes on so quickly." She stared at me. "You're small for your age, Chikul. We named you well." A small smile tugged at her mouth. "Soon the young men will come to court you. That's why I think we should go to Potam."

I didn't say anything. I wasn't ready for that.

"Chikul, I want you to take me to the place where the bones are." Her voice shook a little. I knew what she meant. I nodded. "Now."

"Now?" I asked.

"Yes, I want to see it with my own eyes. I need to know." Her eyes stared far away. "I don't know where everyone is. . . . Where is my mother? Where is Kuta? Where is Kawis? All I see are ghosts."

She scared me. "But, Mother, I saw the bones weeks ago. Maybe nothing's there now." I knew where the bones were: they were deep inside of me, broken and piercing my heart. We walked on our People's bones. We breathed in the ashes of their burned bones. Our dreams clacked with the language of death rattles. But I understood what she meant.

She shook herself. "I will *know*. Take me there!" She got up and handed Paaros to me. I tucked the puppy into the pouch I wore around my waist. We each took a water gourd and set off.

The sands had shifted since I'd been there, and we had to pick our way through the dunes. There were also areas that were marshy, with tall reeds and thick mud. When we reached firmer ground, I let Paaros run. My mother grabbed my hand, and we walked together through stands of mesquite. I craned my neck to keep the puppy in sight, but she didn't go far.

Mother stopped and we sat down to rest. She hugged me and smiled gently. I was so happy to see the light in her eyes again.

"Chikul, my beautiful daughter, how lucky I am to have you!" She kissed my forehead. "Always remember that."

My throat choked up. I hugged her back.

"I want to see if your father's spirit is waiting for me, to see if he has anything to say. Maybe his bones are gone. But I want to say goodbye."

My lips trembled. I was close to tears.

"If you don't want to see the bones again, tell me where to go. You can stay here with your puppy."

"No, I'll come with you. I want to stay close to you."

She smiled and hugged me again.

Under our feet, red stones as flat as tortillas crumbled into sand. We climbed dunes, then dropped down to hard packed mud, then climbed again. Paaros struggled up the dunes, her ears flopping. As we neared the ocean, we heard the surf crashing. Gulls called overhead. We padded across cracked mud. In the spring, the area was a flooded marsh. The dunes rose to the left, blocking our view of the sea. Trees dotted the arroyo. Wild grasses clung to the dunes in thick mats. Ahead was an opening in the dunes where the spring river rushed out into the sea.

Paaros stopped suddenly and growled. It was almost funny, that noise coming from her small body.

Mother put out a hand to stop me. She was quiet. Paaros yipped and ran up over the crest of the dune.

We ran to the dry riverbed where it opened to the beach and stood, shocked.

There were strange people on the beach. Yorim. The white hairy men. I yanked on mother's arm and we hid behind a dune.

"Slave-catchers!" she whispered, her eyes wide in terror. "Run home!"

She pushed me ahead of her. Still weak, she stumbled. I glanced back. Paaros was snarling and snapping at one of the Yorim. The men had gone around the dune and were after us.

I screamed as one man lunged at me, twisting my arm. Another man grabbed my mother around the neck, pulling her down. She bit his arm and he let go. Then he grabbed her long hair and slapped her face. He took down his pants.

Paaros nipped the man's ankles. A third man took his knife and stuck it into my puppy's stomach. Paaros squirmed, pinned to the earth, pawing the air.

The man who held me mauled my chest, pinching my small breasts. I sucked in gulps of air. He pulled me along behind him, over the top of the dunes and back to the beach. I heard my mother screaming.

At the tide line, there was a boat, and more men. One of them spoke to my captor. He had hair all over his chin, even sprouting out of his nose. His hair was yellow like some of our maize. I could see black teeth, and his breath smelled rotten.

He held my chin and turned my head this way and that. He grinned and talked. I tried to twist free, but I was held too tightly. Then he looped a rope around my neck and cinched it. I could hardly breathe.

The men who fought my mother came back to the boat. She wasn't with them. I looked for her, desperately hoping they hadn't killed her. But I knew they had. *Ae!*

I started to wail. A man hit me on the side of the head and lifted me into the boat. My chin hit the wooden sides, and I saw flashes of light in my head. The boat scraped the beach, a wave lifted it, and the men pushed away from shore with long sticks. The water slapped against the boat as we headed toward the largest boat I'd ever seen. It seemed as big as a village and carried a forest of trees on its decks. Huge white cloths billowed from the trees. More men waved from the ship.

The boat fought the surf, then rode the last wave on to calmer waters. I sat at the men's feet, my nose bleeding, my hands tied behind my back, and turned my head toward shore, searching for my mother and my life.

BELLE'S GIFT

Spokane, Washington, 1961

I could be quiet for five whole minutes. If I wanted to. I wouldn't say a single word. Like luminous, pumpernickel, snout.

Mama says I should be quiet. But I like words too much and can't keep them quiet any more than I can stop an orange from squirting juice when I bite into it.

That's what words are for, right? You think of something. Then you say it: *Glass. Celestial. Paperweight.*

Put words together and they make pictures. The sky is a rounded globe where stars twirl around when I shake my head. Mama says I'm too fanciful, but if words could make things change, I would call her Bianca or Eve, and change her fate.

If her name wasn't Meg (*Meg, Meg, gotta wooden leg*), she wouldn't look like a woman hanging up wet sheets on a clothesline, with a mouth wide enough to clamp six clothespins between her taut lips and still have enough room to yell at me. "Clarabel, get down from there this instant!"

Clarabel. My name hangs around me like a cowbell. If I changed Meg's name, my fate would change, too. If she was Bianca, she wouldn't have frizzy red hair that looked like my tattered Raggedy Ann doll. Her hair would be smooth and coiled at the back of her neck, held in place by a shiny barrette. Then I would be beautiful. *Belle.*

I wouldn't have her nose that looks like a petunia just about to bloom. I would be Eve's daughter, and my face would be a perfect oval, like that woman stepping out of a seashell in that painting. My skin would be silky seawater, and my eyes would know how to be coy.

I would change Dad's name, too. His real name is Leif Octavio Jensen. Everyone calls him Leaf Jensen, cuz they don't know any better. You're supposed

44

to say "Life Yensen"; that's the right way to say it. His mom came from Mexico, but his dad is from Denmark. I think his name should be Sven, and he should wear a thick white sweater with little specks of green yarn in it. He should have a helmet on his head with two horns sticking out the sides. He laughed when I told him this.

"It ain't Halloween yet, Jumpin' Bean!"

I hate it when he calls me that, because Mexican jumping beans are just beans full of worms, and that's what makes them move. It's disgusting. It makes me feel crawly inside. He says I just jump around a lot.

When Mama's hanging up the wash, I play on my swing. It's made of metal and squeaks.

"Lord, I wish he'd squirt some oil on that thing," Mama says out of the corner of her clothespin mouth. She looks like Popeye. *Ar, ar.* "You'd think a mechanic could do that in a wink, but you know the old saying about cobblers and their children."

"What's a cobbler?" I yell.

"A shoemaker." She snaps out a bra, puts her fist into the cups to give it some shape, and pins it on the line. She stands with one hand on her hip and stares at the bra. It shimmies in the small wind, sideways breezy breasts of wind filling up the cups.

Behind the thin sheets, worn almost through in the middle in certain spots, I can see Mama's flowers blooming. Along the edge of the garage, she has softened the wooden lines with flags, iris, gladiolus . . . say the word *gladiolus* . . . it makes you glad and full of sunshine. It's a word that means what it says.

I stop swinging. Mama bends over, pulling out another faded housedress from the basket. If her name was Bianca, she would wear silk suits and pillbox hats like the president's wife.

Daisy moos. Her name used to be Cow. One day, though, she ate some wild onions in the pasture and soured the milk. Dad yelled at her. "You do this one more time and you'll be pushing up daisies!"

"Oh, Leaf," Mama said. "She can't understand you! She's a cow!"

"Well, we need that milk." He squared his shoulders. "For little Jumpin' Bean, here."

"Belle." I said.

"What?" He looked at me.

"My name is Belle."

"For chrissakes! You and your fancy ideas. Are you ashamed of us or sumpin'?" He stomped off. "Meg, do sumpin' with that kid."

Mama yelled back at him. "Well, if you made more money, you grease monkey!"

That night I had to be quiet. Mama was mending one of my dresses. It used to be her dress, but she made it small for me. It had big poppies on it. From a distance, it looked like I was covered with giant measles. I sat at her feet, coloring on the back of an old grocery bag. The sky had to be brown, so I just pretended I was living in the middle of a mud puddle. I drew me with my flower nose and my wide mouth with rows of corn kernel teeth. I drew Mama with big hands washing dishes. I drew Dad with fur, swinging from a snaky vine.

Dad was listening to the radio. A big fight. The radio man's voice sounded like a siren, up and down, with a high, excited pitch to it like when you get punched in the guts and are gasping for air and mad as a hornet, and in the background there was a crowd screaming.

"Leaf, that's terrible." Mama pointed with her chin toward me. "Clarabel doesn't need to hear that."

Dad didn't even look at her. He stuck his hand out, waving us away like gnats.

"Big fight." He grunted.

"I like fights," I said. "Jeremy, the new kid, got his lights punched out today after school."

"Oh!" Mama put down her needle. "Was he hurt?"

"Sure!" I remembered the blood streaming out of his nose.

"Boys." Mama shook her head. "They never grow up."

She stared at Dad. He was punching his fist into his other palm, his rear end bouncing off the ottoman. She jabbed the needle into the pin cushion.

That's how Jeremy's nose felt, like a soft pincushion, when I hit him.

That night, I heard something and got out of bed. It was dark and the moon was gone. I saw a faint light coming from the kitchen and crawled down the stairway, one tread at a time, my elbows jutting up like a praying mantis. I hid under the dining room table.

Mama was sliding along the floor in her stockings. Dad was behind her, hugging her really tight. They were playing, I guess. Mama tried to get away, but Dad wouldn't let her. They banged into the cupboard, careened off the fridge, and bumped into the stove. This was a funny game. I stifled a giggle.

Then Dad grabbed a big fistful of hair and shoved her down on a chair at the breakfast table. I frowned. Mama's eyebrows were way up, two birds flying away. She hissed at him like a goose.

"No wife of mine is going to wear lipstick!" Dad pulled out his oily hankie from his back pocket and scrubbed her face. "Why do you need to wear lipstick if you're just going to the movies with Carol?"

He rubbed and rubbed until her lips disappeared. She scratched at his face, crying. I started shaking. Red lipstick was smeared over her cheeks along with car grease and snot. The big hankie erased Mama's mouth. She couldn't say a word. He shook her.

"Huh?" he demanded. "Huh?"

She kept her words inside, all curled up like tiny fists. Her hands fell into her lap. Tears fell on her cheeks as she stared sightlessly over his shoulder at the clock on the wall.

A big fight. Pugilistic. Fisticuffs. Sucker punch.

Dad opened her purse. He found the tube of lipstick. *Red Temptation*. That's what it was called. I know cuz I sneaked a peek earlier when Mama was in the bath. He pulled the lid off and twisted up the red until it stuck out like that mangy dog's peepee. Dad stabbed the lipstick all over Mama's arms. Big red streaks like claw marks. The lipstick broke. Mama sat, her mouth pressed tight. He threw the empty tube into the sink, looked out the dark window, breathing hard. He turned back toward her, rubbed his own cheeks, and sat down. Pretty soon, he was crying, too.

"Meg . . . Meg." He put his head in his hands, sobbing. "Why do you do this to me?"

She got up and left.

I snuck back to bed, got under the covers, and pulled the pillow over my face. I wondered where the moon had gone and why it didn't take me into its darkness, too.

The next day after school, Mama and I drove in Dad's rusty red truck to Quick Pick, the grocery store. As we left, I heard him hammering in the barn. I liked going to town. The store sold gas, kerosene, pig feed, and people feed. I got to ride in the shopping cart. Mama said "Varoooom!" just once, although I begged her for more. She got cross with me, so I pretended my cart was a parade float and I was the princess waving to my subjects.

We got a loaf of bread, a package of bologna, a pound of hamburger, and bananas. I wanted some red licorice, but Mama said NO! She made me walk alongside her, so now I was just a peon, a serf, a little girl with scraped knees. I sulked and she told me not to dawdle.

Mrs. Kooser was at the check stand. She wore her hair piled up on top of her head like a cow pie. She had cat-eye glasses on a leash around her neck. They call them that cuz the frames were shaped like cat's eyes.

I whispered, "Meow."

She ignored me and picked up the bread, punching in thirty cents on the register. Her finger had a wart on it the size of a wad of Black Jack gum.

She stared at Mama.

"What happened to your lip, Mrs. Jensen?"

"Ran into a door."

Mrs. Kooser stopped her warty finger in mid-air. It hovered over the hamburger. I waited for the wart to fall off. If it did, I wouldn't eat the meat, even if it was wrapped up tight in white paper.

"A door." Mrs. Kooser repeated. She looked at Mama over the tops of her glasses.

I looked at Mama's mouth. Usually, I just notice her hands and hips, cuz that's what I see the most of. Her lip was split open with a tiny crusty red pearl of blood on the upper lip. Mama stared at Mrs. Kooser. Suddenly, Mama spun around and left me standing by myself. Two women in the line bent their heads together, whispering and pursing their lips.

Mrs. Kooser tapped her warty finger on the counter. Mama returned, throwing down a tube of *Red Temptation*. "Ring it up."

Mrs. Kooser said, "That'll be $5.85."

Mama counted out the money. Dimes. Nickels. Quarters. She didn't have enough. Her ears turned red. "Put back the bananas," she told Mrs. Kooser.

Mrs. Kooser nodded. The women behind us were silent, craning their necks to see the tube of lipstick as it disappeared into Mama's handbag.

As we left, I heard Mrs. Kooser. "Ran into the door! Did you ever hear such a big whopping lie?" The women tittered.

"Meow," I said and followed Mama out to the car.

Then one afternoon I came home and Mama wasn't there. I gave Daisy a bucket of water and fed the chickens. Feeding the chickens is my responsibility. I'm a big girl. I can dip the soup can into the feed bag and scatter the corn around the yard. The chickens come running. I don't particularly like chickens, though. This is one case where you could call them *Jersey Giants, Dominiques, Leghorns, Chantecler, Rhode Island Reds,* but they'd still be dumb chickens. It's cuz they never look up. They're always pecking at the ground or at other chickens. That's just the way chickens are. You can't change their nature, Mama says.

Once she said we had to have a little talk. She pulled me on her lap. We were sitting outside under the big maple, watching the chickens eat bugs.

"You have to watch out for men," she said.

"Watch them do what?"

She smiled, crookedly. "No, I mean, you're getting older."

"I'm seven, but precocious," I said, repeating what Mrs. Fields, my teacher, told me.

Mama laughed. "That you are." She looked over at her flowers. "See, when you get older, men only want one thing."

I drew back my head. "Only *one* thing?"

She sighed. "Yes, and women want *everything*."

Then she told me a story. It was about Rose Red and Snow White. Not the story with the seven little guys singing hi-ho. This one was about two sisters. One, Snow White, was very nice to an old lady at a water well. The old lady was really a fairy godmother. She gave Snow White a magical gift: every time she spoke, jewels would drop from her lips: diamonds, rubies, emeralds, garnets, sapphires.

When Rose Red went down to the well to get sparkling gems from her mouth, too, she was rude to the old lady, demanding more than her sister. Pearls. Amber. Topaz.

She got a bad gift, instead. When Rose Red spoke, snakes slithered from under her tongue, slugs oozed out between her teeth, and toads hopped out from her throat.

Mama said the moral of the story was to be nice to old women, cuz we'll all be there one day, poor and alone. Men didn't want anything from old women, she said. But when you're young, they want your secret jewel, and they don't care if you look like a toad.

I wouldn't want jewels to drip from my lips. Maybe the prince would only marry me for my riches and not for my vocabulary.

Mama laughed. "Well, just remember. You can't change human behavior."

After I fed the chickens, I sat in my swing. *Squeak. Screech.* I could see the top of the potting shed when I pumped real hard. I liked looking up and up. Today was sky was blue like a robin's egg. Mama had towels hanging on the line, and I pretended they were flags flying from my castle ramparts.

I got off the swing and walked over to the flowers. Mama's gladioli opened their thick lips. *Red Temptation.* Purplish-blue light leaked from the flags. Like yellow butterflies, iris petals floated above finger-thick stalks. I tore off a glad petal and rubbed its redness on my lips. Then I tore off a long blade and tried to sword fight with it, but it wouldn't stick out straight.

Lately, Mama called Dad "The Enemy," as in: "When The Enemy comes home, it's doom and gloom time." Or, "When The Enemy sees this light bill, he's gonna pop his cork."

So when Dad came home, the house dark as a grease pit, he found me watching Tom and Jerry on TV. I stood up with my wilted gladiolus sword.

"En garde," I said, lifting one arm gracefully above my head, half kneeling.

"What?" He looked around. "Where's your mother?"

"Dunno." I jabbed his ankles, the gladiolus leaf hanging from my hand like a dead green snake.

He went into each room, flicking on the lights. There goes the power bill.

"Get ready to pop your cork," I told him.

He squinted. "What?"

The house was ablaze with light.

"Meg?" He wandered around, calling her. He stopped in the kitchen. He picked up a strip of paper, shaped like a fortune cookie paper. It was written in smudged red lipstick. I'd read it earlier.

It said: *You aren't worth it.*

Dad shook the paper. "What the . . ." He read the note again, shaking his head. I didn't get it either.

Who wasn't worth *what*?

He turned the paper over, but it was blank. He shook the paper as if words would fall from its whiteness. Where do words go that are unspoken but felt in the heart? Dad clutched his chest. Then he wadded the paper and threw it on the floor.

He started calling up people.

"Meg there? No, well, guess we got our wires crossed somehow."

"Is Meg there? Okay, just . . . just . . . no, no message."

He ruffled his hair. Finally, he put down the phone. He rubbed his eyes. His stomach growled.

"Hungry?" he asked me, even though it was his stomach making all that racket. Mama says that men don't see things clearly. You have to be very direct with them. Like when you chop off a chicken's head, you don't tell it what you're going to do. You just use the axe. He looked around the kitchen.

"Well, now, where does your mother keep her forks?"

He stood with his hands like two big frying pans, grease blackening the fingernails. I took one hand and led him to the utensil drawer.

"Ah." He held up a fork. Then he got some eggs and washed them, cuz you know where they come from, don't you? He took out a small tub of Daisy's butter. I found the frying pan and put it on top of the stove. It was heavy and I had to use both hands.

Dad stirred the eggs in a blue bowl. Whisk, whisk, whisk. I couldn't be still with that sound. I twirled around, getting scrambled.

Dad fumbled with the stove knob.

"You have to light it, Dad."

"I know that, Jumpin' Bean," he said. "I just got other things on my mind tonight."

"Belle," I said.

He looked at me. His eyes were blue pinpoints of flame. "Where's the matches?"

I showed him. He took a wooden match and scratched it on the side of the little box. Mama lets me have the empty boxes to bury bugs in. Dad held the match close to the burner. Whoosh! Flames shot up like feathers on a rooster's head.

Dad turned down the gas. He poured the eggs into the frying pan. Daisy mooed like a low foghorn.

"Christ." He shuffled his feet, torn between the stove and Daisy's plaintive moos. "Daisy hasn't been brought in to the barn yet?"

"Nope."

"Jesus, do I have to do everything around here? Work hard all day, no dinner, come home to a dark house, and a hungry cow . . . Christ!" He wiped his hands on the seat of his pants and dashed out the door. "Watch the eggs, Clarabel," he called over his shoulder.

"Belle," I said automatically. I watched the eggs. They got black around the edges. Mama did something with eggs, but I don't know what. I shook the pan. The eggs flipped up, then slid out, like big black doilies. They fell between the stove and the wall.

"Dad!" I yelled and ran outside.

He was in the barn, throwing hay into Daisy's manger. *Damnitohell!* I wanted to hear more bad words falling like snails and slugs, but the chickens were fussing. He'd upset them.

"Dad, the eggs fell down."

"What?"

I couldn't see him very well. It was dark. The chickens clucked and squawked.

"Did you feed the chickens, young lady?"

"Of course, I did. They are my responsibility, Dad."

The chickens heard my voice and ran over to me, their stupid heads bobbing. They don't love me. They just want food. They're supposed to be sleeping now, tucking their heads under their wings, but they're stupid. I told you so.

I ran back into the house. I got out more eggs and cracked the shells and put the yolks in the blue bowl. I stirred them. The butter in the frying pan was black and smoking. I turned down the heat. I wiped out the pan with a dish towel. I added butter to the pan, and when it melted, I poured in the eggs. They cooked, clucking.

Dad came back. "Looks like I know what I'm doing," he said, eyeing the perfect eggs.

The next morning, Dad got me up for school. He came into my room and pulled up the shade. It was foggy as milk out.

"Get dressed. We're in a hurry."

I got up. Where were my clothes? Mama always got my clothes for me. Dad said she was visiting friends. But she doesn't have any friends, just me. I felt shaky. In the closet, I found one of those hand-me-down dresses. It was lavender chiffon, from when she went to her high school prom. It was mine, for a special occasion. But we never had any, so I decided today was to be special. Dad told me to come straight home after school, so I wouldn't be able to beat Jeremy as usual. It would be Jeremy's special occasion day. I didn't like what he said about Mama.

I wandered into the kitchen. Dad zipped up the back of my dress for me. I ate corn flakes. I had to find the cereal for him. And the coffee. He drank one cup. His hands were twitchy. He stared out the window a lot. He was wearing his usual mechanic's overalls and his work boots. Mama doesn't allow boots in the house. He saw me looking at them and barked, "Well, she ain't here, is she?"

When I got home from school, I fished out the eggs from between the stove and the wall. I threw them to the chickens. They pecked at the eggs until they'd made a lacy mess. I don't really find it so strange that they would eat their own children.

About four o'clock, I did the dishes. Dad said it was a shame I didn't have more to do, so I had to wash the breakfast dishes and dry them. I put them back on the table, ready for dinner. Dad said he would cook us something great. I didn't know what to do. It was still foggy. I decided to swing.

In the fog, nothing is the same. Mama's towels still hung on the line like spiritless ghosts. The towels, absorbing the fog, had gotten heavy; the line sagged in the middle like a swaybacked horse. As I watched, the clothespins pinged off like wooden grasshoppers, bouncing on the grass. One of her panties fell to the ground. She had a big behind and the panties billowed up like a giant puffball, before slowly sinking down to the wet grass.

I started swinging. *Screech*. The swing's voice tore holes in the fog. I made the swing go faster, and the *screech* ran into itself until I knew it was me, crying.

When Dad came home, the house was dark again. I was cold, shivering, still swinging. He heard the commotion and came outside.

"What in the world?"

I kept on swinging. I was almost going over the top. If I did, then I would go back in time, to yesterday, or the day before, or the day before that . . . to before I was born. Then I could swing back again and be born to different parents.

"Stop that!" Dad yelled. He grabbed my ankles and I flew out of the swing into his arms. We both fell down. I cried and cried. He carried me into the house like he used to when I was little. Before I got old and had Responsibilities.

We sat in a pool of light in the living room. One light in a house full of darkness. He held me.

"Listen, things are going to be a little tough for awhile." He stroked my hair. I wanted to suck my thumb, but I was too old for that. "Your mother is off finding herself."

I lifted my head. "How can you lose yourself?"

Dad whispered. "You don't know you've lost your dreams until you wake up, and then it's too late."

"I thought she was visiting someone," I said in a small voice.

He didn't say anything, just held me and rocked me.

"Jeremy, the new kid, said she was at a sleepover with Mr. Shipsky."

He stood up abruptly and I slid off his lap. "He did, did he? Well, he's wrong. The kid's wrong."

"Dad?"

"What?"

"Is Mama coming back?"

He got his coat and shrugged his big shoulders into it. "That ain't the question."

I frowned. "Well, is she?"

"Better question is, why would I want her back?"

"Dad!"

"Sorry, Jumpin' Bean." He sat back down. I looked at him carefully. Usually, he was far away, high up, like the statue of the dead soldier downtown that the pigeons mess all over. Now I could see the bony ridge above his eyes, his dark Indian eyes. And his mouth had two lines going down from his strong nose. His hair was almost blond, but there was a blackness inside the gold strands somehow. His cheekbones were high and the warm brown skin was flecked with freckles. I heard women say he was handsome.

He cleared his throat. "See, your mama and I are mad at each other. We had an argument, I guess. I don't know what's going to happen next. Your mother . . ." He shook his head.

I twisted up my mouth. "I always know I'm going to hit Jeremy the new kid."

He looked at me. "You hit a boy?"

I nodded. "Sure."

"You're not supposed to hit people."

"You and Mama hit each other."

He hung his head. I tugged at his sleeve, but he ignored me, brushing my hands away. "Your mama, your mama," he finally said. "She's got me by the cojones."

"Jeremy the new kid said you don't have any or you'd get your wife back."

Dad's mouth dropped open. "He said what!"

I shrugged. Of course, I knew what cojones were. Sometimes grown-ups are too dumb for their own good. Dad looked pretty pale. He didn't say anything more about me hitting Jeremy.

We went to Quick Pick. Dad looked at the hamburger, shaking his head. He moved over a bit and stood in front of the steaks. "Ah, what the hell." He grabbed a package of T-bones.

Mrs. Kooser's leashed glasses were resting on her bosom. Mama says that's a good word to know, "bosoms," because it's proper and polite. It's not nice to say "breasts." So sometimes when we eat chicken, I say, "This is good chicken bosoms." Mama rolls her eyes.

But Mama's not here. Just Dad and me and the T-bones, two baking potatoes, a pack of Miller's. The bottles clinked merrily. A party sound. He got some potato chips and guacamole. "All your basic food groups," he said. "You got your greens." His finger poked the guacamole. "You got your starches." He jabbed at the potatoes. "And your proteins." He pointed to the steaks. "And you got your liquids."

Mrs. Kooser clicked her nails on the counter. "Say, Leaf Jensen, where's the missus lately?"

I could feel him trembling. The cat's got his tongue.

I spoke up. "She's visiting her sister."

Mrs. Kooser tilted her head. "I didn't know she had a sister."

"Her name is Aunt Bianca."

"Bianca." Mrs. Kooser scratched her arm with that warty finger. It looked like the wart had a finger instead of the other way around. She smiled at me.

"And where does this Aunt Bianca live, little girl?"

I sucked in a deep breath. "In a house, of course."

Dad found his tongue. "How much do we owe you?"

She looked at me strangely but answered Dad. We paid and left the store. On the way out, we heard someone calling Dad. It was Mrs. Perillo, who had been standing in line behind us. She caught up with us, huffing and holding one hand across her heaving bosom. The other hand carried a bag of food.

"Leaf Jensen!"

Dad nodded politely. "Mrs. Perillo."

"Now, maybe you don't know this, but you cook those potatoes for an hour at 350 degrees, all right?"

Dad chewed his lip. "I can bake a potato, I guess."

"I'm sure." She nodded down at me.

He thanked her just the same, and we walked away. She cleared her throat. "If I should happen to see Meg, is there any message you might want to give her?"

"No," he turned away and then back again. "Yeah, tell her that her daughter is worth it." We got into the car and roared out of the parking lot, leaving Mrs. Perillo shaking her head in a cloud of exhaust.

Dad said, "Thanks, Belle, for your quick thinking with Mrs. Kooser."

"Belle," I corrected automatically, and then gasped. Mama always told me that you can't teach men new things, you can only train them through constant diligence. I guess she was wrong. Dad learned my name. I felt bad about her being wrong and me being glad that she was.

At home, Dad started the oven. Popped the taters in. It was too soon to cook the steak, he said, so we might as well start on the Or Derves. He handed me the chips and guacamole. Poured himself a tall beer. I gulped down some black cherry Kool-Aid.

"We ain't doing so bad for ourselves, are we?" He mussed my hair. Pretty soon, he finished a beer. Knocking over the empty bottle, he said, "There goes another dead soldier."

After a bit, he cooked the steak. I liked to chew on the bones, smearing my cheeks with grease. I grinned up at him. "We're just a couple of grease monkeys, aren't we?"

He laughed with me. There goes another dead soldier. We eat more chips. Dad said it's time for bed. He read me a story, which is a novel experience, pun not intended, and tucks me in. He left the door ajar, and I heard more dead soldiers falling, rolling, next to their fallen comrades, helmets clinking in a dead soldier salute. Then I was falling, falling, deep into sleep. Next thing I knew, a cannon went off. Boom!

I ran out. Dad was in the kitchen in front of the open oven door.

"What happened, Dad?"

"It's the darndest thing. The potatoes blew up!"

We peered into the oven, like Hansel and Gretel, and there's the witch, sticking to the oven in a hundred pulpy pieces.

"Oh," I said. "Mama usually stabs the potatoes first."

"Go back to bed." He rolled up his sleeves, burping, and swaying slightly. "I gotta clean this mess up."

The next day, after Dad milked Daisy, he took me to school. We waved good-bye. I didn't do anything in school all day. I don't know why they make us come. Lunch was okay. I forgot to punch Jeremy after school.

When I got home, Mama was waiting for me in the living room. She was wearing a pale sapphire-blue suit with shoes that matched, and a purse small as a blue pancake. I stopped so suddenly that the screen door hit me in the rear.

"Oh, you've grown!" Mama blurted out. She took out a small white hankie and dabbed her eyes. She wore Red Temptation. Her hair was blond like summer wheat, and smooth as Daisy's flank. She had sooty black stuff on her eyelashes. She smelled like a bouquet.

"Zsa Zsa?" I asked her. She looked like that actress.

"What?" Mama wrinkled her nose. She stood up and held out her arms. I ran to her and she gave me a big hug. My eyes got hot.

"Mama!"

Slowly, she pulled away. "Oh, dear, what am I going to do? Oh, dear."

"Well," I said with my hands on my hips, "you can clean out the oven where the witch blew up. And the dishes aren't done. You don't know how hard I work all day, and I'm tired! Damnitohell!"

Mama's eyes widened.

There was a knock at the door. It was a man. I scooted behind Mama and peeked around her hips.

"Margaret?"

"Tucker, I need more time."

He opened the door and stuck his head in. He saw me but didn't say anything. His eyes darted all around like a heat-maddened fly. Finally, he settled on Mama. "We're going to miss . . ."

"I *said* I need more time." She took a deep breath and turned to me, while telling him to wait in the car.

His head popped back out. He stomped off the porch.

I wondered what they would miss if she stayed with me. I wondered if she'd miss me if she left. I buried my head in her lap. She soothed my forehead, brushing her soft palm across my brow.

"I just can't do this, I just can't. I can't leave you." Her voice was ragged.

She pushed me away and went to the door. I held on to her dress like a baby elephant following its mama. She opened the door and, in tandem, we stepped out onto the porch.

"Tucker!"

He got out of a shiny Red Temptation car. He stood behind it, looking over the top, one hand resting on the car roof. He was dark-haired with blue eyes and a caterpillar mustache. He had dimples. Smiling, he waved for her to come on. "Hurry, dear." Then his smile faltered. She stood next to me with her arm around me.

"Tucker, I can't leave my daughter. You've no right to expect that."

He drummed his fingers on the roof. "Well, then, bring her along." He smiled weakly.

"I gotta talk it over with her daddy." Mama rubbed the center of my back where she said my angel wings used to be. "You go on home now."

"Margaret!" He started around the car, but she slammed the front door. She twisted the lock firmly. Her forehead rested against the door as I clung to her skirt, my hand wadding up the rich material.

Dad came home and there was no dinner on the table, just a stack of limp bologna sandwiches. Earlier, Mama had wandered from room to room, sighing. When I reminded her about dinner she just shook her head, as if it didn't matter.

"Everything looks different," she marveled. "Nothing is mine anymore."

I wrote my name in the dust on the hall table. *Belle*. Even in dust it was a lovely name. My name. A name that sounded like a bell and beautiful and exotic. Not like an old farmhouse with shadows in every corner.

"Oh, you don't understand," she said under her breath. "But I've only been gone five days and there's no connection any more . . ."

She stopped suddenly, groping for the living room sofa. "What does it mean?" She sounded scared as she plopped down. "This is not my life anymore! After ten years on this farm with your father, I'm a stranger in my own life."

"Did you lose your dreams and wake up?" I repeated what Dad said.

"My God!" She took my chin in her hand and looked into my eyes. "Aren't you the smart one!"

So when Dad walked in and saw the bologna sandwiches drooping pathetically . . . and probably teeming with little armies of Salmonella . . . on the plate, he dropped a dead soldier onto the floor. It rolled under the table. I tucked my feet out of the way. Mama and me were doing my homework. She fidgeted and sighed a lot while I rubbed out the answers, trying to subtract three numbers. A father, a mother, a child. Take away one and what is left? A big fat zero. I sniffed a lot.

He was shocked to see her. Before she said a word, she held up a hand like a traffic cop. "Not a single word, Leaf, until later." She meant when I was in bed. Dad plunked down a bag of groceries. The soldiers rattled their sabers. I resolved to stay awake. I wouldn't miss this for the world. My world.

So I trotted off to bed when I was told to. Then, after I could hear Dad was done eating the steak he burned himself, I sneaked out. Under the dining room table, it was dark and the chair legs hid me like a forest of polished saplings.

Dad was leaning against the kitchen counter, strangling a beer bottle. Mama was standing with her back to the fridge, the table between them.

He crossed his legs, casually, and asked, "What are you doing here, Meg?"

"Margaret."

He rolled his eyes. "Not you, too." He took a gulp of beer. I watched his throat work. It looked like there was a giant toad stuck in there.

Mama spoke. "I came back to talk to you." She took a tentative step towards the table and held on to the back of a chair. "I couldn't take you anymore. All this fighting."

He grunted. "What, I'm not fancy enough for you like that Fucker Shitsky?"

"His name is Tucker Shipsky and there's no use talking to you if you take that attitude."

"You want to shack up with Shitsky and let the whole town know about it, and all you care is my *attitude*? Kee-rist, Meg." He set the bottle on the counter. "Look at you, all made up like a Hollywood whore."

"We're not shacking up. He's just a friend helping me through hard times." Mama lifted her chin. "And I look nice."

He took a deep breath. "No wife of mine will wear cheap lipstick and sleep around with a shoe salesman!" His voice trembled. "Meg . . ."

Mama laughed. "You're so predictable." But the laugh turned into a sob. "So maybe I'm not your wife anymore, Leaf." She leveled a look at him. "And he *owns* that store."

His arm shot out suddenly, sweeping the bottle into the sink. It clanked and rolled.

Mama pressed forward. "Look at you! You drunken injun wetback!" Her words shot out like bullets. He staggered backward.

His eyes glistened with tears. "Don't call me that. My grandfather escaped from the Mexican federales and walked all the way up from Guaymas. He was only a kid."

"And he died a drunken Yaqui injun in Long Beach, staggering down the road at three in the morning." She put her fists on her hips. "I don't care about him. I don't care that the Mexican army was killing your people! That's ancient history. I'm talking about *now*. You're a pathetic drunk."

"I drink because . . . because you . . . want things and I give what I can and it's never enough." He sniffed. "I do the best I can, Meg. I gave you a home and a kid and a life."

58

"Is that what I wanted?" She glared at him.

He frowned, bewildered. "But . . . you said . . ."

Her laugh was harsh. "This was the life *you* wanted, not me. You wanted to live like a white man like your dad . . . who, I might add, left you and your mom when you were a kid. You wanted to be a real American with a nice little farm . . ." She sniggered. "And a white picket fence, which I might add, is falling down." She swung her arm out, pointing. "Think I like living on a farm, stepping in chicken shit? Think I like making Belle's dresses from my cast-offs? Think I like having a dirty wetback for a husband? Think I like a husband who wants me to look ugly so he doesn't have to worry I'll flirt with the tractor salesman?" She snorted. "And is this the life you really wanted? You're a drunk grease monkey with no ambition. Sure, you're good-looking. I see you looking in the mirror at yourself, turning this way and that. But you're still a violent, drunk man without any substance."

His legs slid down and he sat on the floor, his mouth open. Mama advanced around the table, relentlessly attacking.

"You're not worth the ground Tucker walks on."

Dad blinked. "But . . . I love you, Meg. Even when you hit me and made fun of me, I loved you. I gave you my life."

"For what that's worth," she said, her lip curled in disgust. "You aren't much of a man, Leaf, for all your Mexican machismo. Your balls are the size of a Chihuahua's."

He stood up quickly, shaking his head as if to clear it. "Stop it, Meg."

"No, I won't. I came back to get Belle." She crossed her arms as she stood in front of him.

His face paled. "No! You can't take her."

"Can and will," Mama taunted him, sticking her chin out.

"But . . ." Suddenly, his mouth hardened. "You want balls, Meg? Okay." He lunged at her, grabbing the lapels of her beautiful jacket. Her high heels scrabbled on the floor, ankles twisting as he dragged her to the sink. "Scrub off that lipstick!"

She caught herself on the counter edge. They were inches from each other's face. She spat at him. The saliva dribbled down his lips.

"You think I'll be the old Meg if my lips are bare? Huh? Huh?"

He reached out one hand and twisted on the tap. Water gushed out. "It's a start, honey."

"No."

"Can and will," he mimicked.

"Fuck you, Leaf." Tears were streaming down her face. I was barely breathing.

59

I was scared but it seemed like I was watching a Wile E. Coyote cartoon. One catastrophe after another, and they kept bouncing back. Beep! Beep!

"Wish you would." He purred, his eyes like slits. "You never liked doing it much, did you, Meg? Always told me I was pathetic in bed. So how does Shitsky like it? You putting out for him? Well, I'll show you how to grease my monkey, you bitch." He squeezed her bosom.

She aimed a kick at his shins. It connected and he gasped, releasing her. She stepped back, groping for the drawer. She pulled out her rolling pin as he rushed her.

She raised her arm and conked him on the head. He teetered like a dead soldier, a funny surprised look on his face. Then, knees wobbling, he slid down, his back to the wall. His eyes rolled up and he fell over.

"You killed him!" I screamed, running into the kitchen.

Mama dropped the rolling pin. "Oh, God! Leaf?" She knelt. "He's not dead. He's not. He can't be." She looked at me. "What are you doing out of bed, young lady? March right back!" She ran her fingers through her hair. Pins tumbled out and the neat blond hairdo fell apart. "Shoo! Shoo!"

"Mama!" I stood my ground. She didn't even see me. She was muttering to herself.

"If he's not dead, he should be," she said.

A trickle of blood ran down Dad's face. I leaned over and put my ear to Dad's chest. He was breathing. "Mama . . ."

She had already gotten up and grabbed a flashlight. She kicked her heels off.

"Mama!" I tried to tell her he was alive, but she ran out the door. I yelled after her that he was breathing, but she just kept going. I pried up one of Dad's eyelids. He was out cold, like Jeremy the new kid. This would never have happened if Dad paid better attention to what was where in the kitchen.

Mama barged back in. She stood over us, hands on her hips. "Got the wheelbarrow and shovel, Clarabel. I'm gonna be busy for awhile, so you do as you're told and go to bed."

"But he's still alive!"

"He can't be." She knelt down again and placed her hand over his heart. "Oh! Man's got a head hard as his heart." She rocked back on her heels. "Well, he *is* dead. You just don't understand these things."

"No, he isn't! Mama! I can feel him breathing!"

"Residual air in the lungs, that's all."

"But his heart is beating."

"It's just your own heart echoing in your ears." She tucked a strand of her hair behind her ear.

"But Mama!"

"Will you be *quiet*, Clarabel, for five damn minutes? I gotta think." Her eyes took on a faraway look as if death was just over my shoulder. I turned around as the hairs on my neck rose. When I turned back, she was up and dragging Dad across the floor by his ankles. She grunted and swore.

I grabbed Dad's head and tried to stop her, but she was strong. She planted her stout legs and wide hips and pulled and pulled. His back bones cracked as I wrestled, trying to pull him back my way. I couldn't do it. I crawled across the floor, cradling Dad's poor head from any more bumps. I crab-walked, angry and scared.

I kept calling her but she ignored me. She tugged him across the porch and stopped, panting, at the steps. Her chest heaved.

"I can't live with this man anymore," she admitted, her voice raspy. "Lord knows I've tried. I tried to be a good wife. To fix his meals and wash his clothes. Raise his kid. Iron his shirts."

"I thought men only wanted one thing," I reminded her.

"What?"

"Dad just wanted you to love him."

"You don't know anything, Clarabel. You're just a kid."

"Belle." Why couldn't anyone remember my name? Why did she list me with ironing and washing clothes?

Mama sat back on her haunches. "I gave him the best years of my life. Now I see what I missed. I didn't know . . . I didn't know I could expect more from life." She looked at me in wonderment. "I thought I had to settle."

I frowned as she went on. "Your daddy is a handsome man. He turned my head, that's for sure, but there's more to a man than good looks. Money is important. You, Clarabel, deserve more than this." She waved a hand vaguely at the yard. "I left my family for him. He said we'd be rolling in dough. We had so many plans! How'd we end up here?" She shook her head, confused. "Clarabel, this is my chance. Yours, too. You're coming with me." I saw her tongue, wet and sluglike, wiggle in her mouth.

I couldn't breathe. She wanted me to leave Daddy! "No! We can't leave Dad! He blows up potatoes and can't make my school lunches, and he doesn't know how to fix my hair." He needed us.

She stared at me for a long time like I was crazy. Then she stood up and grabbed Dad's ankles again.

"Mama?"

Dad moaned. She dropped one foot and closed her eyes. "Clarabel, go to bed."

"No."

"Look at me, honey." She leaned closer to me. I smelled damp earth rising around us. The wheelbarrow looked like an upended snail behind her. "I'll let it be your choice." She nodded curtly. "Yes, that's what I'll do." She glanced at Dad. "Do you want to come with me?"

I gulped, confused. What was she asking me? There was something snaky behind her teeth, and its eyes glittered in her dark mouth.

"Mama, you can't . . ."

She put a finger on my lips. "Can't you be quiet for just five minutes and *think?*" Her lips whispered their Red Temptation. "What I do will depend on what you say, Clarabel, so be quiet and think carefully." Her eyes darted to Dad, who lay half on the steps, his breath ragged. At the bottom of the stairs, a shovel leaned, its handle a faded red.

I looked at the night sky. I could hear Daisy's hooves on the stall floor, and the chickens awakened by the barn light Mama had left on rustled their feathers, clucking, and complaining. The big maple was full of leaves and the shapes of stars. Shadows seeped out from the shovel and Dad's mouth and Mama's heart.

Across the sky there was a darkness beyond my reckoning. No words could describe how it formed a long river that twined its dark ribbons into the earth. I felt my breathing slow and heard Dad swallow. Mama sat so still, like a pale moth under the porch light, her skin edged in its sinister yellow light. Her breath fluttered as she stared at me.

I looked around at our farm. The sheets still hung on the line, like a herd of tired and moldy cows, their immense flanks flat in the rising moonlight. The gladioli had fallen over with their heavy burdens; the top-heavy flowers bent the stalks in half, those red lips choked with earth.

Everything was different. I turned my hands over, until the palms flashed up at me. I was helpless in the silence. Without words, I was nothing. And yet, I couldn't give her the words she wanted.

If I could be quiet for just five minutes, I would remember something I once knew before I knew words. Something more important than answers.

If I could make my choice . . . staying or going . . . in these five minutes, I would know what I needed the most, not who needed me the most. I could know that words were a choice that only the living have. I looked at Dad. I looked at Mama. I started to open my mouth. She shushed me.

"Be quiet and think, Clarabel. There's no going back with your decision." She didn't look at Dad or the shovel. Her eyes bored desperately into mine.

If I could only be quiet for five whole minutes, diamonds of minutes, sparkling and glittering like precious words! If I had the gift given to the good girl, then my answer would be a jewel.

PAINTED LADY

After her husband left her, Meg came to me looking for work. I knew her, of course. She's bought all her bulbs and flowers from us for years. She's got ten green thumbs. I told her I'd talk it over with my sister, Liv, and get back to her.

I almost didn't recognize Meg. She'd dyed her hair sunflower yellow. She wore tulip red lipstick and lots of mascara. I noticed her fingernails were long and painted crimson. She wore pedal pushers in mint green and a short white blouse. If she worked for us, she'd better get used to chipped nails and old Levis.

Our nursery is a small operation. A few acres, a greenhouse that needs a new fan, test beds, a small warehouse, and potting sheds. We specialize in iris, glads, and plants that attract butterflies. Brilliant yellow yarrows, native to Eastern Washington, grow on the prairie our grandfather first farmed in 1899. Just before Meg's rusty truck crunched up the gravel road, I'd been looking at a Painted Lady breakfasting on the nectar of wild yarrow. We call our place "Butterfly Gardens."

Behind the old barn, you can see our grandfather's sod house. He came from Denmark and dug out a house ten feet by ten feet. He lived there all winter, alone. In the spring, he emerged, blinking and bearded like a cinnamon bear. He was a little crazy, so we come by our dispositions naturally. Even when he got married to a Swedish girl, my grandmother Inge, he preferred the sod house to the wooden one he built for her.

He claimed to hear the roots growing in his earthy chamber and the staccato hoofbeats of deer on the roof. Inge could never budge him or cajole him to spend the whole night in their bed. They had four kids. My dad was the youngest. When he died, Liv and I inherited the farm. No one else wanted it.

Up on the high prairie, the sky is a deep marvel. You can drink in the air, gulping mouthfuls that taste like cold flowers. It's flat land jutting up like a mesa from the surrounding woods and creeping suburban plots. Before Grandfather Bjørn cut the sod, wild onions and sage covered the virgin land.

I suppose there were Indians around here once. There's an old trail that bisects the prairie. Last year, some kids digging a fort found old bones. The police came out and said they were from an Indian over a hundred years old. He was folded up like an old lawn chair, roots binding the bones together. They gave the body back to the local tribe, the Spokans.

Five Mile Prairie has good soil, sweet and rich. We live on the northwest part where the pines seem to grow taller. We're three hundred miles east of the ocean, but Grandfather must've felt that the waves of wild grasses reminded him of the Baltic Sea.

When he died, we buried him in the sod house. Liv says it's like the old Viking burials, where chieftains were buried under mounds shaped like their dragon ships. Instead of copper torques, white horses, slaves, or battle axes, we buried him with a bottle of aquavit and his Danish/English dictionary. Through the years, we've adorned his grave with other things; two beaters from mother's mixer, the crumbling rubber from a dead tractor tire, the wicked tines of a gaping tiller. You might think it's all just junk, but it isn't. It's what's left of our wealth, once-coveted objects, now worn and rusted.

Farms don't pay off nowadays. We don't have thousands of acres, knee deep in loess, like they do on the Palouse. They farm wheat and lentils there. The farmers are rich. But not us. One winter night when the ice was an inch thick on the window panes and we were burning whole forests of trees, trying to keep warm, Liv and I sat down.

"Something has to change, Erik," she said to me. We talked, drew diagrams, argued, and finally went to bed, each of us dreaming in our own bedrooms of summer as the wind battered the house. We had the same dream. Grandfather was combing butterflies out of his long beard.

Butterflies. In Danish, it's *sommerfugler,* or summer birds.

We were eating a breakfast of home-canned cherries and cornbread. Last night we had cornbread and canned peaches. We were sick of being poor. After my truck broke down and I was laid off at the railroads, we ate too many beans and canned fruit. I knew I could find work in the spring. I'm big and strong, but no one was hiring right now. Liv wasn't the marrying kind. She huddled with me, slurping cherries and spitting out the pits.

"So what does the dream mean?" I asked. "We're supposed to raise butterflies?"

She shook her head. "Let me think a minute." Finally, she looked at me. "What if we have a plant nursery? More and more houses are being built. They need plants. We can do the usual stuff, like petunias and junipers, but what if we grow plants that butterflies like?" Her eyes shone with enthusiasm.

I raised one shoulder. "I don't know, Liv." Then I shrugged. Why not give it a try?

And so Butterfly Gardens was born out of desperation, a kind of failure we Andersens had cocooned ourselves in for three generations.

That week, the weather broke and the sky lifted. Liv and I walked out to Bjørn's grave and sprinkled cornbread over the tangle of his beard. We told him about our dream. He thought about it a long time while birds flew down and groomed his beard. His silence was agreeable. We knew we had his approval.

Now we have too much work. We sure could use Meg. I found Liv digging up some Japanese roof iris. We already planted some on Grandfather's roof, thinking he'd like the purple flowers blooming over him like stars. Irises originated in China. We bought some from a specialty catalogue years ago and found it fitting to bury one immigrant over another. Liv was putting some tender muscle into the digging. It has to be done carefully. You can't hack away or the bulbs will be damaged. It takes strength, too, to lift up the dirt-clogged mass of roots. Each plant dies at the end of a season, multiplying only at the crown, where a new shoot appears, kind of like Athena from Zeus's head.

Liv had already topped the foliage and trimmed the roots. I watched her as she shook soil loose. When she was ready, I turned on the hose and rinsed the roots. We worked silently together.

Liv's a lot like Mom. She's strong but wiry and kind of small. She doesn't talk much while she works. She gets really focused on the task at hand. When we stopped for a break, I told her about Meg.

"You're right, Erik," she said. "We need help. And she's good with plants."

"I know." I frowned.

"What, then?" She waited, knowing I had something on my mind. Wisps of blond hair curled around her face. Her sea-gray eyes regarded me patiently.

"She's selling her place. Can't afford it now that her husband left." I grabbed an empty burlap bag. We needed to pack three dozen irises for Mrs. Scott. "You probably heard about what happened."

"Everyone's talking about it at the grocery store," she agreed. "Well . . ."

Liv smiled. "You want her to move in with us?"

"There's an idea." I pretended to be surprised at her suggestion.

She laughed. "You like her?" She could read me like a book.

I shrugged. "I don't really know her, but . . . why not?"

"She's got a kid. I've met her a few times. She's a little 'different.'"

"Guess she'll fit right in, then," I said. I looked at her. "What about you, Liv? Do you like Meg?"

"Sure." She bent over, giving me a view of her rear. I grinned as I saw her ears tinge with pink. Like I said, Liv isn't the marrying kind. Not that she doesn't know about love. There was Carol last year, but she was sulky, and Liv needs someone less dormant.

Living among flowers makes us believe that there's beauty in all forms. Meg certainly captured my attention. Liv was even more susceptible than I, knowing something about the roots of female beauty.

"They can have the back two bedrooms," my sister said as she straightened up. So it was settled.

They moved in a month later. It was late spring and their cow, Daisy, was turned out into a large pen. I'd spent some time shoring up some old rotten beams in the barn and fixing the corral. They brought their chickens and a bald rooster.

Meg got a room facing west where she could enjoy the sunset. Belle got a room with a big maple tree near her window. I saw her open the window and yank off a new leaf. She measured the leaf against her hand. Then she placed it under her pillow. She looked at me. Her eyes changed color. Sometimes they seemed dark blue, and other times I could see flecks of green and brown and gold. She had dark hair with glints of red and gold. Nothing seemed permanent with her. One moment she was solemn; the next she was circling the room like a dog getting ready to lie down. I left her to get used to her room.

It was late evening and the sky was still light to the west. I walked out to chat with Bjørn. I felt eyes and more eyes watching me. Maybe the deer that had stepped on sage, releasing its pungent scent. Or the bats that flickered high above, scooping up insects that floated on updrafts.

Old Bjørn was restless. I could feel sheet lightning through the soles of my feet. I squatted down, chewing on a blade of grass.

"How's it going?" I put my palms on the earth. "What do you think about our new boarders?"

Silence. My grandfather's wisdom was best summed up by him staying out of our lives. It was we that wouldn't let him be, to rest in peace. I'm not crazy enough to expect an answer from him, but he does answer in his own way. We can hear it in our minds. He gives variations of silence that only family members can interpret. Grandmother Inge was very good at it, having plenty of practice while he was living. Now she's buried in the Christian cemetery south of town.

I stayed out there a long time. Saw a comet. Then I wandered back to the gardens. Tall columbines were just forming their buds. There were pale bluish-purple heads of globe thistle, asters, daisies, petunias that filled the air with sweet aromas. I knelt by Test Bed #1. Three years ago, I started a new kind of iris. It's white, bi-color, with a creamy throat. There was a ruff of dark magenta and a deep yellow eye zone. I was following in Schreiner's footsteps, developing a new flower by increasing the set of chromosomes. In my case, I first noticed Iris #1 after a hard frost. The extreme cold affected a Britannia, which made a hybrid with Paper Moon the following summer. If you want to get a true seed, you need to cross-pollinate the plants yourself. I'd never done that before. First I had to contact the American Iris Society. They gave me permission to try. Then I pored over books, studying the process.

With sexual propagation, you need to use two of the same species. Remove an anther from the flower, using tweezers. Scrape the pollen from the anther onto the stigma of the next plant, the female. Carefully tear the outer petals from the female. This prevents a bee from cross-pollinating with an undesired male plant.

It's a tedious process, technical sex, without the beauty of bee or butterfly, but it's the only way to breed true. Sexual propagation is a process, not a feeling. It's not love that makes the world go round.

When the plants are ready, we transplant them into beds. My new flower was doing well. There was a lustrous quality of light seemingly transmitted by the flower itself.

I like the night. I looked up at Meg's window. The dark square absorbed the starlight. I imagined her breasts rising like two moons. She excited me with her wide hips and beautiful face.

Liv's room was below Meg's. The light clicked off. The window was open. If I stood close, I could probably hear her restless sleep, the mutterings of a lover's name or scraps of dream words. I wonder how much she's attracted to Meg. I want Meg, too, and it suddenly hit me that we've been foolish to invite her into our house. We can't cut up our desire and divide.

I spend too much time with flowers . . . their smell and vaginal shapes, my hands dusted with pollen, roots shaped like penises, petals like parting lips.

I'm reminded of something Linnaeus said about sex: the sexual attributes of plants "we regard with delight, of animals with abomination, of ourselves with strange thoughts."

OWL WOMAN

The night my daddy and mama got into a big fight and she hit him with the rolling pin and I squawked like a plucked chicken was enormous with its sounds: the wheelbarrow creaking, a car door slamming, a man's big voice hushed, all the flowers the color of dried blood.

I fell asleep with my eyes open.

And later, when Mama came into the room, I was really asleep, but I felt her eyes on me and her sour breath, and I wondered if in her nails the blood and dirt were small seeds sprouting parts of my daddy.

The next morning the sun was bright as a penny. She said, he left me.

Why?

Because he didn't care, Clarabel. I saw her strange face: eye stacked over eye, brows crawling like maggots . . . face like a broken mirror, with all her teeth strung around her neck. I cried.

Now. Now. It's only a bad dream, she said.

I didn't wake up until we moved out to the farm with Liv and Erik.

Daisy came with us. She liked her new pasture, but the chickens were afraid of the barn. It smelled like owls.

I got a new bedroom with leafy shadows on the walls, and outside there's a tree with its valleys of smooth silver wood where the rain drips down. Tribes of crows huddle in the tree like old men without their umbrellas. Each night, for weeks, the crows came and talked, their eyes polished stones. Sometimes they wickedly jabbed at each other when lies were told. At night the tree was the color of salt in the moonlight. I sleepwalked among them, my toes curling like claws. Each leaf was a map of the sun and wind. I took leaves to bed with me, scattering them across my bed, spanning my hand against their arches, and then I slept. I was safe in a green cathedral.

My tree is the center of the world. The wind lives there. It is the oldest tree in the world and has bits of teeth and feathers and blood in its center. At night I hear voices from the tree. Tiny fetuses push against the bark, swelling out a foot or a horn.

Bjørn teaches me all I need to know. Erik introduced me one day, and I like to sit on Bjørn's house and talk to him.

I never *dream* about my daddy anymore. He's in Valhalla, the heaven for slain heroes. Bjørn says I should remember my daddy in the sky and clouds. Like God, my daddy is everywhere and in everything.

Other times, I *think* about my daddy. How he knocked over the dead soldiers. How he let me wear a silk dress to school. How he fell after Mama hit him, and his eyes were closed, but underneath the lids he was dreaming about riding off with a Valkyrie. Mama asked me that night who I wanted to live with, but I never had a chance to answer. He was gone and there was a sound of metal ringing in the night. Was it a sword or a shovel or the car door slamming? I remember Daddy holding me in the dark room when Mama was gone and how his arms were warm and safe.

If she killed him, then the police would've taken her to jail. But she's still here, so he can't be dead.

Yet he's not here. Mama says he doesn't care about me, but I know that's not true.

Mama gave me a little book. It's a thesaurus, so I'm learning new words to keep the ravens awake at night. *Abandonment. Sorrow. Forgetfulness.*

One evening, the sky was lit by heavy clouds the color of sulfur and coal. Wind blasted down the chimney, and Liv closed the flue, cursing in Danish, *for satan!* Up in my room, I sat with my chin on the windowsill, watching the ravens climbing on top of each other, desperate to hug the trunk. The leaves whipped around, a nest spiraled to the ground, and I saw lightning burning the air, forking like an upside-down candelabrum. The whole house shook from thunder. There were bells of clouds and then a silence before the rain came.

I was so excited! The smell of rain and sweet grass in the air! I ran outside, ignoring the shouts of the grown-ups. I ran into the wet. The rain, hard as diamonds, polished me. I fell down on Bjørn's grave, laughing until my sides ached.

One day I asked him if he doesn't get tired of his small house.

"Oh, no, child. It is wery large."

I looked at it. A house made of blocks of earth and an old blue door Erik had propped up as a joke. A broken wheel at each corner so it looked like the house could roll away. A house for broken things: a toothless rake, a battered milk can, Bjørn's bone bed. It looked small to me.

"Death is bigger than all of us, child!" He sat on his roof, waist deep in blue iris. He wore a long red cloak and leather kilt. He told me about Inge, his wife.

"She's buried vith those damn Christians." His cleared his throat. It sounded like rain going down the gutter pipes. "Vun day she vas knitting in her black dress. She alvays vore black the last few years, anticipating her vidowhood. She yust knitted the minutes avay. Even ven she cooked my dinner, her hands pulled at the ball of yarn. But then vun evening, it vas twilight, and she dropped a stitch. Oh, my, she said, and vas dead."

"That's terrible," I said.

"Och, no, for she vas already dressed for her own funeral!" Bjørn laughed until *his* sides hurt.

It made me think of Daddy, and I didn't laugh. I don't understand God or Death. It doesn't seem funny to me.

Liv said God is a woman and showed me a picture of a woman statue with about a million bosoms. To feed all of life, she told me. I think of Daisy. Mama said Daisy is about a hundred years old in human terms. Her milk is thinning. I watched her lick the reddish salt block and knew she was as old as God. Erik said God wears a dark suit and is a Lutheran with a pulpit on every cloud. Everyone laughed.

Mama said God doesn't exist. After we die, that's it. There is no heaven. When Daisy dies, she turns to dust and bones.

I don't want to think about Death anymore.

At night, Erik brushes Liv's and Mama's hair. He divides the hair into roots, combing out dust and pollen until he says his fingers are heavy with the fertility of earth and flora.

Mama is Liv's best friend. They hold hands, heads bent over lilies. Liv is teaching me about flowers. Mama pins tiger lilies in my hair. They're orange with spotted petals and long tongues. We listen to fiddle players on the radio and dance in the greenhouse, our elbows knocking against buckets and empty pots.

I wonder if Bjørn is lonely out by himself, but Liv says he's probably visiting Odin and drinking mead from skulls.

Everywhere you look there's death.

I like to walk on the prairie. One morning, the clocks were ticking too loud. I went outside while everyone was still sleeping and decided to converse with Bjørn. But just when I got near his house, I saw him shuffling over a hill, wearing an old coat. I ran after him but he was too fast. I flew down the trail and, suddenly, there he was.

71

"Uh hun hah," he snuffled. I sat down. He was a big bear.

"You smell bad, pee-uuu!" I held my nose.

He swayed his head, looking at me with small, dim eyes. Then he ambled off.

I followed his tracks. They were as big as Erik's feet. At last I came to bedrock covered with lichen. An old woman waited for me.

"You talked to that bear," she said. She wore a flowered cotton ankle-length dress. Her white hair was in braids tied with red cloth, and her head was covered by a red scarf. She leaned on a cane. In the other hand was a basket.

"My name is Humishumi." She smiled. Her face looked like tree bark. I liked her.

"My name is Belle. It means 'beauty,'" I said.

"My name means 'mourning dove' in Salish."

"What's that?"

"It's an Indian language."

I frowned. "Erik says there're no Indians left around here."

She twisted her mouth. "Well, but I am here and you, too."

"I'm not Indian!"

She eyed me. "You look like it." Then she looked across the prairie. "I used to come here when I was a little girl. My family came here every spring to dig up *quamash*."

"What's that?" I asked again.

"You call it camas. We dug up the purple-flowered camas and ate the bulbs. Never eat the white-flowered ones. They're poisonous."

That was interesting. We sat down for awhile, and she told me stories about when she was little and about stick people and dancing. I helped her up. She said she had to go.

"Where do you live?" I asked her.

"In my memories," she said softly.

One night I woke up to the sound of Owl Woman hooting in the tree. Mourning Dove had told me all about her, too. Her Indian name is Sne'nah, and she eats children.

I hid in the branches of my wooden bed under my feather pillow. I peeked out with one eye.

Owl Woman had tufts of hair in her ears and big round eyes. She said to me, "Come out, little chipmunk."

"No!"

Owl Woman shook her beak. It clicked. "Come out. Your father wants to see you."

"My father is dead," I said, my heart beating too loudly.

"Then your mother wants you," she said.

"My mother is sleeping." I was glad to catch her in her lies.

"Well, then, your auntie wants you."

"I don't have an aunt." I covered my head.

"Then it must be your grandfather, little chipmunk." Her beak clicked again.

I peeked out from under the covers. Maybe Grandfather Bjørn did want me. "Close your eyes, Owl Woman, and I'll come out."

I climbed out of bed and tiptoed down the stairs.

There were lots of stars but no moon. I looked around and saw Owl Woman swooping down toward me. Run, run. Hide! I ducked under the old washtub. My toes stuck out. I called for Grandfather but he was snoring.

I was shaking so much the tub rattled against my head. Owl Woman cackled on the fence post. I smelled the chickens' fear.

From the far end of the pasture, a coyote howled. Owl Woman called to him. He trotted up and they joined forces. His Indian name is Sin-ka-lip. I remember Daddy telling me about Coyote's Indian name, and it was different. It was Wo'i. So maybe I am Indian, cuz he was. I wonder how many kinds of Indians there are. And how many names for everything?

Maybe Coyote has as many names as Death.

"Smell out the little chipmunk," ordered Owl Woman. "We'll both eat her."

Coyote sniffed at my trembling mice toes. He opened his mouth.

Then Mourning Dove charged at him with a firebrand. She burned his nose, which is why it's always black. She threw fire at Owl Woman, who can't see when there is light. She gnashed her beak and screeched, flying away.

I hugged Mourning Dove. The sun was rising, full of flames. Then she sent me back to bed. When I woke up, I remembered the Owl dream and I was scared. I ran out to the tree.

At the base there was an owl pellet. It was made of soft hair, and a fingernail poked out. I remember Owl Woman saying, "Hmm. So good. Little girls' hearts are the best."

The pellet was too small to hold my broken heart, my useless broken wheel of a heart.

A SINCERE PROFESSION

Catherine Reynard was a pretty girl with large brown eyes and plump cheeks. She sang as she dried the dishes or folded laundry. She wore designer clothes, had a pair of diamond earrings, and twenty-six pairs of shoes.

And she was poor.

Or so she believed because her father told her so. "We're the working poor," he said. He explained that it meant he could give her nice things, but they couldn't afford a yacht or a membership to the country club. She didn't understand. But she nodded and didn't worry about it anymore.

Warner thought you told kids only what they could understand. So he didn't tell her much. She was sweet and not rebellious like most teenagers. Her mother would've been proud of her, bless her soul.

Every day he went down to Colby Avenue and sat on a street corner with a large piece of cardboard. Written in dark marker, it said: "Sick vet. Please help."

Warner wore old jeans with holes at the knees, a faded Pearl Jam T-shirt, and a baseball cap with the word "ARMY" on it. His toes stuck out of his sneakers. His hair was ragged and greasy. He limped, favoring his left leg.

He made a lot of money. On average, he made almost $100 a day. His favorite day was Sunday. He stood humbly in front of a church and caught the folks as they entered, when they were more pious and generous. Even with the downturn in the economy, he did OK. People felt even sorrier for him. If they were struggling, what was this poor guy going through? So, his income was down to $60 a day . . . sometimes even less . . . but it was steady.

He didn't get a vet's pension, because the closest he'd been to a war was when he was eight, playing with his G.I. figure named Sgt. Victor. It was now his alter ego.

Sometimes, he'd take a working vacation and drive down to Pike Place Market in Seattle. The tourists loved seeing the colorful characters there, from the fish-throwing fishmongers to the street musicians with their open guitar cases. He'd bring out some balloons and make wiener dogs or giraffes for the kiddies. Parents laughed and forked over lots of money. After all, they were on vacation!

He'd amassed quite a chunk of money through the years. He had a savings account, a CD account, and some money hidden away under the porch. Warner believed that beggars had a profession like anyone else. You had to dress for success. You had to understand human psychology. You had to accept bad weather when the rain dripped down your nose or when the sun broiled you batty. Beggary was no different than being a big-shot account exec. You had to be tough and resilient. One of the advantages was that no one could fire you. And you never had to wear a tie.

Or you could say beggary was a calling. People needed to feel virtuous. They needed to see someone lower in life than themselves. They needed to know that at least things hadn't gotten as bad as that poor guy.

Sure, some people lectured him.

"Get a job!" they'd yell out their car window.

"I'm not giving you any money," they also said. "You'll just spend it on drugs or booze."

But that was part of the job. People in the 9 to 5 life had to put up with crap from their bosses, coworkers, or the public. They just couldn't walk away like he could. No, this was what he was meant to be. Warner was sure he had it all figured out. He had a daughter at home who cooked and cleaned for him. He had self-respect, knowing he earned his daily bread in a sincere, if not entirely honest, way.

And then one day he came home and Catherine was giggling on the porch with a young man. His name was Jason Brown. He trained as a realtor, but the recession had hit him hard, so he worked as a part-time office assistant for a window company.

Catherine and he had been seeing each other for some time. It wasn't exactly a secret she'd been keeping from her dad, but she hadn't talked about it, either. She was nineteen and knew she needed to get out of the house. Life was beckoning to her in the shape of a six-foot-tall, grey-eyed young man. When she introduced Jason to her dad, she was a little nervous. Warner had just come home from work, and his hair needed washing.

Catherine knew her father was an entrepreneur. She was proud of him having his own business. Something to do with marketing. But she wished he didn't have to dress like that. He told her he dressed down so his clients wouldn't feel intimidated. Most of the clientele were in some kind of trade.

Tonight was the big night, Jason thought. He was going to ask Mr. Reynard for his daughter's hand in marriage. It was kind of old-fashioned, but Jason thought it would be a nice thing to do. While Catherine was getting the dinner ready, the two men sat in the living room. Warner took off his dusty hat and placed it on the coffee table. He stretched out in the lounger and folded his hands over his stomach. It had been a long day, a bit windy, and his eyes were irritated. The young man who sat across from him on the sofa looked soft. He fidgeted. Warner sighed. The youth these days weren't up to his standards. Not at all. Sure, this guy looked clean. But you could tell he had no street smarts. He was like all the rest of the suckers in the world.

He was gobsmacked when Jason leaned forward and laid out his plans.

"Sir, I'd like to ask your permission to marry Catherine. I've got a job . . . well, two jobs. Eventually, this recession will end and things will get back to normal. I'll make enough money then to provide for anything Catherine would ever need or want." Jason blushed. "And when the kids come . . . they'll have the best of everything."

Warner sat with his mouth half-opened. Why hadn't he ever seen this coming? Not just this yokel with an earnest expression on his baby face, but the fact that one day, Catherine would leave?

He let out the breath he'd been holding. He heard pots clanging and water running in the kitchen. She was playing the radio and singing along. Did she know what this yahoo was up to?

Imagine him marrying Catherine! And him proud of having two jobs! If you were smart, one job was all you ever needed!

Warner rubbed the stubble on his cheeks. Maybe what this guy needed was a lesson in the real world. Hard Knocks, Inc.

"Yeah," he said slowly. "You can get married but you have to join me in my business for six weeks."

Jason smiled. Wow. Her dad must really be impressed with him. He looked around, noting the big-screen plasma TV, the leather sofa, the recliners, and crystal glassware in the armoire. Her dad must be very successful. This might be the big break Jason needed.

Warner leaned closer, darting a glance at the kitchen. "But you can't whisper a word of this to Catherine."

Jason frowned. *What the . . . ?*

"You have to dress like a poor man. Get out of that suit, man. Get some scruffy clothes."

"I don't understand." Jason was baffled. Was this a joke? But as Catherine's father talked more, he began to realize that her dad was serious. He was very confused. Finally, he asked, "So, you're a panhandler?"

Warner reared back, insulted. "No! I ask the public for socially responsible contributions. I am an important link in the local economy."

Jason blinked. "You hold a sign and sit on a street corner. That sounds like a bum to me."

"If you continue to insult me, then get out. And never see Catherine again." Warner put on a stern face.

Jason shook his head. "She's over eighteen, sir. We'll just elope. We don't need your blessing." He was angry. "I've got a job. I don't need to beg."

Warner shifted forward again. "You know that Catherine and I are very close. Ever since her mom died, we've been like this." He held up two crossed fingers. "If you make a rift between us, it'll kill her. She'll hate you for it."

Jason stood up. "No way. She loves me. I'll just tell her what you've said, and she'll hate you."

Warner stood up. "I doubt that. It will just hurt her. You know how sensitive she is."

Jason knew that. She practically worshipped her daddy. He didn't know what to do. He was mad and confused.

"Why? Why do you want me to do this? I don't get it."

"You need to know how hard the world is. I need to know you love my daughter so much you'll do anything to take care of her."

Jason shook his head again. "But beg? I can't do that. Tell Catherine I have a headache and need to go home."

"Tell her yourself, boy."

Three days later, Jason found her dad on the corner of Hewitt and Rucker. Jason pulled over to the curb and walked back. Warner was slouched, holding up the cardboard to his chest, shoulders dejected.

What her dad said was true. He didn't know about life's difficulties. He'd gone to college, majored in business, taken his Realtor's test, and then waited for the big sales to come. But the recession took down the housing market. His own dad had gotten him the job at the window company. He was young and had confidence in his future, but heck, this might be kinda fun. When he wasn't working at Clear Glass, he could make a little extra cash this way. It'd be like acting. He'd been in the drama club in high school, and it was fun.

Without any preamble, he said to Warner. "OK, I'll do it."

Warner nodded. "Take a dollar . . . no, make it a ten . . . out of your pocket and hand it to me, OK? Smile and pat me on the back. It'll encourage the drive-bys to roll down their window. Kind of like product endorsement. OK, so then walk away. I'll meet you around the corner on Hoyt in five minutes."

Jason stared at him. Then he reached for his wallet, pulled out a ten, and did what Warner told him to do. He slapped on a fake smile and walked away. He got into his car and drove around the corner. He spotted Warner coming toward him and pulled over. Warner got in.

"Now you need to learn the ropes, kid, so listen up." Warner angled in the seat so he could face Jason. "Go to the thrift store and get some old duds. Not too bad. You wanna look poor but respectable. You can't look scary or people will stay away. Make sure your shoes are old too. Lots of newbies make that mistake. You gotta be the whole package. Think of a story. Are you a vet?" Warner shook his head. "Nah, you don't have the look. OK." He thought a moment. "Maybe you're sick. No, you look too healthy. Well, let's keep it simple. You're out of work like millions of others. You got a sick mom to take care of. You . . ." He stopped. "Aren't you writing this down?"

Jason looked at him blankly. "What?"

Warner rolled his eyes. "Get it down, for chrissakes! I'm training you, kid."

"I don't have any paper."

"Go buy some. There's a drugstore down the street. And get a pen, too. You don't got one of those, do you?"

"No." Jason shook his head.

"Well, what are you waiting for?"

"I don't have any money. I gave you the ten."

Warner gave a long, exasperated sigh. He leaned forward and dug out his wallet. "Here. And get me a cup of coffee while you're at it. Tall, cream, no sugar."

Jason looked at him. "Uh, okay. Wait here, I'll be back."

"I ain't going anywhere. Look, it's starting to rain. You better get a leg on." As Jason got out of the car, he called out. "And you'll owe me that ten."

Jason stopped and turned back. "What! That was my money!"

"And you gave it to me."

"You told me to!"

Warner shook his head. "No, I asked you to and you did. Completely voluntary."

"But . . . but . . . it's my money!" he sputtered.

"So now you're robbing a beggar? How low can you go?"

Jason was speechless. Warner made shooing motions with his hand, and Jason left, slamming the door.

Stupid kid. Warner chuckled. Kids these days. Didn't know a thing about life and what it meant. It was pathetic. What did they teach them in school anyway? Nothing practical, that's for sure.

Lesson number 1, kid. Don't trust no one.

Two days later, Warner met Jason by Safeway. Jason was wearing old jeans with a baggy seat, a white T, and a blue windbreaker. Warner circled him.

"T-shirt is too white. Throw it in the washer with some black clothes. Windbreaker makes you look like an FBI agent. Take it off."

"But it's cold!"

"Good. It'll make you look even more pathetic."

Jason gritted his teeth. "This is ridiculous!"

"What? Too hard for you, baby cakes?" Warner sneered. "Can't hack it, can you?"

Clenching his fists, Jason kept his temper. "I can do anything you can."

Warner laughed.

"And better," said Jason.

Warner slapped his thighs, laughing so hard tears came to his eyes. Jason turned away, mad as hell.

Finally, Warner wiped his cheeks. "You're a hoot." He cleared his throat. "OK, let's get on with it." He pointed down the street. "See those guys over there by the post office?"

"Yeah."

"Don't go near them. They got a table set up, and they're trying to get votes to impeach the president. They got his photo up on a big ol' sign and put a Hitler mustache on him. They're a bunch of kooks. People will pull into the parking lot, see them, and get mad. They won't be in the mood to donate money to your bank account."

"Uh, OK."

"Where's your sign?"

"In the car trunk."

"Well, get it out, boy."

Jason opened the trunk. It was a big Rainbow Realtor sign he'd covered neatly with typing paper that didn't completely hide the colorful sign letters underneath. In block letters, he'd written "Help sick Mom unemployed."

Warner guffawed so much he almost wet his pants. "Kid, you're priceless," he finally gasped. "Didn't you learn any punctuation in school? It should say "Out of work. Family needs help."

"But you said my mom is sick."

"That's your background story, kid." Warner was patient. "You gotta have a story."

"Why?"

"Cuz some well-meaning do-gooder will come up to you one day and want to know your life story."

"I'm only twenty-two."

Warner grinned. "So make it short and sweet." He gestured at the sign. "Get some cardboard, kid. That looks like you're campaigning for Gay Pride."

Jason blushed.

"Say," said Warner. "You don't happen to really have a sick mom, do you?"

Jason shook his head.

"Too bad. Too bad."

Warner directed him to the liquor store. In the back, there was a pile of crushed cardboard boxes. They quickly took one and tore off one side.

"Now write what I told you."

"With what? I don't have a pen."

"Jaysus!" He put his hands on his hips. "Buy one then, chump!"

Jason walked away, wondering how it could cost him so much to pretend to be poor.

For four weeks, Jason worked alone on various corners during his off hours. He divided his days up into two parts: office clothes and bum clothes. He began to resent his time at the office. People telling him what to do. The boss ordering him to redo the invoice files. The measly pay.

On the street, he was his own boss. He learned to wear a hat so no one would recognize him but was kind of surprised when one of his friends drove by and didn't know him. No one wants to really see the poor, he realized. It scared them. No one wanted to be the next one holding up a sign.

At first, not many people stopped to give him money. Warner told him, move away from the bus bench, you idiot, and stand by the intersection.

Still, most people didn't give him anything. Two guys in suits came by and offered to buy him a meal and take him to church. He mumbled no, he couldn't eat a thing, knowing his family was home hungry. They gave him a couple of bucks and a church magazine that said God was coming soon.

One man offered him a job raking leaves. He was bored and did it. Warner scolded him for not seeing the bigger picture.

"You think you made money by raking, but you didn't."

Jason frowned. "I made twenty bucks."

Warner shook his head. "You went for the immediate pleasure of making twenty and didn't look ahead. You could've made double that hustling." Warner knocked Jason on the head. "Hello? Anyone there?"

Another time, Jason met up with Warner at the park. It was a nice day. The sun shone over the Sound, and the water sparkled so brightly that Jason's eyes watered. They sat at a picnic table.

Jason counted out his money. He'd made $80 that day. Warner had made over a hundred.

"You're doing good, kid. Not as good as me, but I've been in the business for twenty-five years." Warner yawned. "Nice day, huh."

Jason stuffed the bills into his wallet. "Don't you ever think that what we're doing is wrong?"

Warner sat up. He brought his fist down on the table. Jason jumped.

"Wrong?" He leaned forward, intense. "How are we wrong? What about all the bankers who stole everyone's money and started this recession? Or the mortgage lenders that ruined the housing market? Did they care about you and your job or the thousands of people who lost their homes?" Warner glared. "No, they didn't. What we do is straightforward work. We ask for money and we get it. Or we don't."

"But . . ."

"But nothin'. Be thankful you got this job and a corner to stand on. Not everyone is that lucky." His voice softened. "And, kid, I think you're finally getting it. You're making good money. You got the knack."

Jason felt proud of the praise. He did have the knack. He made more on the street than he did in that crummy office job at minimum wage.

Another two weeks passed and Warner told Jason to meet him at Blarney's after work. It was a nice neighborhood bar. It was the end of summer and little tables were set outside under umbrellas, but it was getting a little colder, so most of the patrons were inside. Jason was used to bad weather now, though. His skin was tan and his legs were stronger from walking the streets.

Warner came to the table carrying two beers. He sat down across from Jason and eyed the young man. He'd come a long way.

After a few swallows, Warner started talking. "Jason, you did what I asked, and now I'm ready to give you my permission to marry Catherine. Stop working on the streets and concentrate on your real estate career. Times are getting better. I read that house sales are up. Well, the prices are down, but people are ready to buy. You'll do well and take care of my daughter, I know." He gave Jason a gentle punch on the shoulder.

Jason pursed his lips. He sat silently, took a sip of beer, and then spoke. "I like it on the streets. No one tells me what to do. I can make my own hours. I made more the last month than I did for two months at the office." He shook his head. "No, I don't want to stop begging."

Warner sat there, astounded. Finally, he spoke. His voice was quiet. "I used to feel like you. But think about your children. It hurt me to lie to Catherine. She still doesn't know what I do. Are you going to keep it a secret from her, too?"

Jason stared at him. "So, what are you saying? I thought you said we did a public service, that it's a job like any other."

Warner squirmed uneasily. "It is. I'm not ashamed of my profession. But I want something more for my daughter."

Jason drained his glass. "Man, I don't want to go back to the rat race."

"Then you can't marry Catherine."

Jason laughed. "Guess I don't want to marry her bad enough to be locked up in a cubicle for the rest of my life." He shoved his glass. "You taught me to be independent, dude. I don't want to give up my freedom for a picket fence. A cage is a cage." He stood up. "I've changed, dude." He threw a couple dollars on the table. "See you around."

Warner sat there for a long time after Jason left. Life never turned out the way you expected it. It confirmed what he'd always known . . . that you took what you could when you could.

He scooped up the tip Jason had left and pocketed it before sauntering down the street.

CHOICES

Jessica Corbie was married to Elijah Corbie, a young man who fancied himself a rapper. He spent most of his time every day hooking up with his friends, Sam and Bobo, and with Jessica's brother, Justin. They all trooped down to Sam's parents' basement and sat around drinking beer and trying out new songs.

Bobo beat time on his thigh as he rapped.

"That was lame," jeered Sam.

"Dude," said Bobo after the others laughed at his latest effort, "life is lame."

Sam rolled the beer can between his palms. He made a grimace. "Life sucks."

"And then you die," said Elijah.

They were quiet for a few minutes. Justin mumbled, "You guys got any money? We could go rent a movie."

Bobo stood up and pulled out the lining of his pockets. "See any money?" He plopped back down on the old sofa.

"We should do something." Elijah got up and paced the paneled family room. It was furnished with old furniture and a foosball table Sam got for his twelfth birthday. Two of the little figures were missing their heads. A dartboard hung on one wall, but there were no darts. A radio with a tape deck sat on a dusty bookcase.

"Do what?" asked Bobo, listlessly.

"I dunno know. Something."

"Like what?" Sam picked at a loose thread on the sofa.

"I dunno, I said," replied Elijah. "Do I gotta do all the thinking around here?"

"We could go hang out at the mall," suggested Bobo.

Justin sneered and spoke in falsetto. "Oh! Oh! Let's go hang out at the mall with all the high school kiddies."

Elijah laughed.

Bobo's cheeks flamed. "Well, I was just saying . . ."

Elijah sat down again. Everyone looked at him and waited. He was their leader, always coming up with ideas. Some of them were crazy, like the time he got them all to hop the freight train to Seattle. Bobo almost slipped and fell under the slowly moving wheels. Elijah had pulled him up at the last second. And then there was the time he goaded them all into a scavenger hunt. They had to shoplift items from a list. Bobo was the only one who chickened out. He "suddenly" felt sick. He was almost voted out of their gang, but he brought them a bottle of tequila and they let him stay.

They weren't much of a gang. They liked to call themselves the Snakes. They practiced drawing snakes on their biceps with blue ink. They couldn't afford to get real tattoos.

They were twenty-one and considered legal adults, but none of them were self-supporting. Elijah's wife, Jessica, worked as a cashier at a dollar store for minimum wage. They ate most of their dinners at her mom's house. Jessica was a hard worker. She wouldn't have married Elijah, but she'd been three months pregnant when they were married by the justice of the peace. She lost the baby a week after the hasty wedding.

Elijah looked up suddenly. He snapped his fingers. "We need money, right?"

The young men nodded.

"Where do you get money from?" he asked.

Bobo spoke up. "Work."

When the guys stopped howling, Elijah jabbed a finger to his forehead. "Think!"

Sam shrugged. "My parents go to the ATM."

Elijah beamed. "Very good. You're close."

No one said anything. Justin was worried Elijah was thinking of something very, very illegal. Finally, he said softly, "The bank?"

Elijah stared at him like he was crazy. "What, you think we should rob a bank?"

Justin shrugged, trying not to look confused.

Elijah leaned forward, putting his elbows on his knees. He lowered his voice.

"Do any of you morons think you could rob a bank, even if you wanted to?" he asked.

Bobo gave a little laugh. "Nah. We're too stupid."

"That's not the answer I was looking for, Bobo, but coming from you it makes perfect sense."

Bobo frowned, trying to work it out.

"So what, then?" asked Sam.

Elijah sighed. "*I* could rob a bank, but you guys are too stupid." He held up a hand as Sam protested. "Think about it." The guys did and had to agree. Elijah was clever in a way they didn't understand. He went on. "They got cameras."

"We could wear disguises," suggested Sam. The others nodded.

Elijah ignored them. "They got panic buttons at every teller station. The cop shop is only a quarter mile away from the bank. They put dye in every stolen packet." He looked at them. "No. The bank is out."

"So . . . ?" asked Justin.

"Soooo," said Elijah, grinning, "we rob Duke's." He sat back to watch their faces. Bobo looked blank but that was nothing new. Sam frowned. He was a thinker but only on the surface. Sam was repeating Elijah's words in his mind, trying to find the meaning behind them. It would take five minutes.

Justin cocked his head and nodded. "Duke's. That might work."

"Are you serious?" Bobo squeaked. He shook his head. "They don't got no money."

"Dudes, I've been thinking about this a long time. They're a regular money machine." Duke's was a mom-and-pop grocery and liquor store. "We sneak in the back on a Sunday morning when it's closed. Duke doesn't take the weekend money to the bank until Monday, cuz the bank is closed on the weekend, see?"

Sam and Bobo nodded. Justin grinned. "Yeah," he said. "They must be rich after all that booze sold on Friday and Saturday nights!"

'But we'll go to jail if we're caught," said Bobo. He was nervous.

"Bobo, you're a genius," said Elijah.

"I am?"

"Yep. You pointed out the major problem in any robbery: getting caught. So the solution is *not* to get caught." He smiled. "And we won't. They don't have any cameras, cuz I've been throwing rocks at the one in the back for two months now. I overheard Duke saying he couldn't afford to replace it again. I broke four cameras!"

Bobo put his fist in the air to give a high five, but nobody paid attention. He dropped it back down into his lap. The others were mulling the idea over.

"OK, so we go in the back," said Justin, "and then what? They got a safe."

Elijah shook his head. "Not really. They have one but don't set it, cuz old Duke can't remember the combination. I know that for sure cuz I used to work there, remember?"

Sam nodded. Elijah had bagged groceries last summer until he was fired for turning up late or not at all.

"When do we do it?" asked Justin. He tried to look cool, but he was nervous, too. He could see Bobo rocking back and forward a little. Sam was biting his lip. Elijah wore his stone face.

"Tonight," Elijah said.

Bobo shook his head several times. "Can't! I can't!"

"Why not?" asked Sam. "Is Baby Bobo afraid?" he taunted in a singsong voice.

"It's Mom's birthday."

All the guys sat still, barely breathing. Finally, Elijah nodded. "You're excused."

Bobo's mom had anger management issues. Once, the police came to investigate a noise disturbance. She was arguing with her third husband. She got so mad she threw the sofa through the living room picture window, narrowly missing a cop. Her second husband wanted to enter the Witness Protection Program to get away from her. She couldn't afford a dentist, so she got her cousin Nick to pull out a bad tooth with pliers. She liquored up and sat back in a chair. He pulled the wrong tooth, and when she found out, she went after him with a gun. She winged him in the hip. He moved to Montana.

Everyone was afraid of Mama Michelle.

Bobo relaxed. He even smiled a bit, but it faltered at Elijah's next words.

"You gotta get your mom's gun."

Bobo paled. He shook his head. "I can't."

"We gotta have a gun."

"Why?" asked Bobo.

"Cuz we got an image to uphold. We are the Snakes!" Elijah said. He made his fingers into fangs and hissed. Everyone did the same. It was their sign. Privately, Elijah thought it was dumb, but the dudes needed something to rally around.

Bobo shook his head again. "I can't. At night, she sleeps with it under her pillow. During the day, she . . . uh . . . puts it there." He patted his chest. "I ain't sticking my hand down there!"

Elijah rolled his eyes. "OK, but we need a gun. Who has one?" Even as he asked, he knew it was a stupid question. These guys wouldn't know a gun from a gumball.

No one said anything. He sighed. "Fine. I'll get it myself." He looked at each one of them. "No one blab about this, understood?" He waited until each of them nodded, and then, after a few more words from him, they all went home.

"Cool," whispered Sam as Elijah showed him his uncle Jack's gun. It looked like a gun from an old cowboy movie. It had a black rubber grip. When Elijah was a kid, Jack had shown him the gun, handling it carefully and not allowing Elijah to touch it. His uncle kept it locked up in a cabinet in the den. What Elijah didn't know was that the gun was a collectible. Fewer than twenty thousand of the Ruger .22 caliber Single Six were made by 1955. Elijah knew where the key was hidden. He'd been a sneaky little kid.

Last night, he stopped by his uncle's place. Jack was getting along in years and didn't get out much. He was glad for company. After a few beers, though, Jack had to head to the bathroom. Elijah got the gun and bullets, stuffing it all into his backpack.

Now the Snakes stood in the alley behind Duke's. It was five a.m. and dark out. A streetlamp shone at the mouth of the alley, but it was dim where they were. Sam wore a black hoodie. He glanced around nervously. Justin kept yawning.

"It's too early to get up," he complained. He wore a black hoodie, also. It was their gang colors.

"I never got to bed," said Sam. He yawned, too, and rubbed his eyes.

Elijah groaned. "I told you to get some sleep." He rolled his eyes. "OK, well, you ready?"

Sam scuffed his shoe on the gritty pavement. "Why we all got to go in? I mean, won't it be too crowded?"

Elijah mulled it over. There was some truth to that, but sticking together made it more like gang business. Everyone was guilty that way. It made him feel stronger. He shook his head and pushed Sam toward the door.

"I got stomach cramps," Sam protested. It was true. He was shaking. He'd never done anything like this before. Why'd he let Elijah talk him into doing this?

"Fine," Elijah sighed. "Stay out here and keep watch."

"Okay!" Sam practically danced. "I'm the lookout."

"C'mon." Elijah motioned to Justin. Justin's mouth was dry. He nodded and followed Elijah.

"I got a pick from Duecey," said Elijah. Duecey was a small-time burglar. He'd tossed a spare lockpick to Elijah without any questions and gone back to the racing form.

Elijah bent close to the lock, motioning for Justin to shine the keychain minilight on the hole. As Justin leaned closer, his shoulder touched the door. It swung open.

Justin looked wide-eyed at Elijah, who paused before cautiously opening the door.

"Old fool must've forgot to lock it," he whispered.

They crept down the dark hallway. Justin felt the hairs rise on the back of his neck. He didn't like this. Something wasn't right. He *knew* things sometimes. He couldn't explain it. His grandma said it was his Yaqui native heritage. There's lots of ways of knowing, she told him when he was younger. Now he felt danger. He reached out to touch Elijah's elbow, but Elijah turned the corner.

They stopped outside the office. It was a cramped, windowless room used for storage and a desk. The safe was in there.

Justin opened his mouth to speak, but Elijah was already turning the doorknob.

He followed him inside.

They both stopped abruptly. Three men were there, bent over the safe. One held a flashlight.

At the sound of the door opening, a tall man pointed a gun at Elijah.

"What the . . . !" The voice was rough but familiar. Before Justin could identify the voice, the man raised the gun.

Elijah tried to pull out his gun, but it got caught on the hoodie pouch. His finger fumbled and he pulled the trigger.

The gun bucked and he yelped as the barrel burned his finger. A man fell down, hit by the bullet. Sam screamed and swung a broom he found by the door. It hit the tall gunman on his wrist, and the gun fell. It went off, the bullet hitting the man who lay wounded on the floor.

The second bullet was fatal.

The other two men jumped Justin and Elijah. There was a fight. Elijah struggled but was slugged in the jaw and went down. Justin saw stars as he was hit on the head.

Outside, Sam heard gunshots and ran off.

Jessica liked sleeping in on Sunday morning. Her days off were Sunday and Monday. She stretched in bed and turned over, suddenly aware that Elijah was gone.

She sat halfway up and called softly, "Hey?"

It was too quiet. She got up and pulled on a sweatshirt over the tee she slept in. She wore flannel pants. She put her feet into her slippers and walked out into the living room/kitchen. It was a small place. The tiny bathroom had a shower and toilet, no tub. It was called an efficiency apartment. Jessica could barely afford the rent on her income.

Elijah was gone. She had a sinking feeling. Something wasn't right. When she heard a quiet knock on the door, she almost didn't answer it.

She stood in front of the door and took a deep breath. "Who's there?" she said.

"It's me, Zack."

She frowned. She'd dated Zack back in middle school. Her first love. Slowly, she opened the door.

He was a big, tall man now. His brown eyes were fierce but softened at the sight of her. He bit his lip.

"I'm here on Los Locos business, *querida*."

She frowned. "I . . . don't understand."

He put a hand on her shoulder. "You have to come with me."

"Why? Now?" She wrapped her arms across her chest.

"Just come." He still liked her. She was sweet and pretty. She stepped back. His hand tightened. He added, "It's about your man and Justin."

Her eyes widened in fear. "What?"

"They got into some trouble. You got to come."

She stared at him wordlessly. Then she grabbed her purse and followed him.

Los Locos had their headquarters in an old building down by the river. One of their relatives kept it for storage for his boat business. He let them use it whenever they needed it, thinking the gang was more wannabe than real. He figured it was like a clubhouse for men who'd never grown up. They could play their poker there or whatever. What he didn't know was that they were into robbing and car thefts.

Inside, thin light seeped in through grimy windows set high in the walls. Jessica stood in front of Elijah and Justin. Both were tied up with their hands behind their backs, sitting on chairs, gagged. Elijah looked at her, scared. Justin had his eyes shut tight until she spoke. Then he opened them and pleaded with her, wordlessly.

"You gotta choose, Jessie," said Arturo. He was the leader. He stood behind the men. "They got Alejandro killed. Someone's gotta pay."

Elijah tried to talk through his gag.

"Choose?" she said, confused.

"Both of them killed him. They both should die, but outta respect for Zach, we thought you could save one." Arturo liked Jessica, too. She always smiled at him when she saw him on the street. He remembered when he was younger and she put a Band-Aid on his scraped knee. She'd wanted to be a nurse, but then . . . life took over.

"I can't choose!" She was horrified. "How can you expect me to do that?"

"Better to lose one than both," added Zach.

She closed her eyes. Her grandma, Alma Luz, once told her that Yaquis knew how to face life's hardships. It was part of their creation story. Those ancient people who couldn't face the future were allowed to leave the human race.

Some ran into the desert and became ants. Others waded into the waves and became dolphins or sea mammals. Only her ancestors decided to face life. They did it with wisdom and courage.

She took a deep breath and squared her shoulders. She knew Los Locos meant business. She had to choose.

She looked at Elijah. She had fallen for him. He was funny and cute. But he was awfully lazy. Then she looked at Justin. He was her brother. He didn't like to work, either, but she had lots of good memories about their childhood.

Both of them stared at her. There was only one possible answer.

"Well?" asked Arturo.

"Take Elijah. I can get a new husband anytime," she said calmly. "But I can never get another brother."

JAY (DEVIL-MAY-CARE!)

It doesn't take long to learn to speak like a human. My tongue is used to warbles and screeches, caws and alarming imitations of hawks. So, the human language (English, to be precise) is only a minor variant of cacophony. Words can transform, cover, and reveal.

Of course, my transformation left me naked as (excuse the sly humor) a jaybird. My feathers lay in a shimmering pile at my toes, which looked like grubs. I had to stop myself from bending over and eating them. I wiggled the toes, experimentally, and the sheen of feathers winked in the shaft of a forest sunbeam. I stepped forward, crushing a feather. The blue (O the sky!) bled out into the air. Blue is transient. The day sky is full of darkness, only we don't see it. Oh, I'm not much of a philosopher. I'll leave that to the Great Ravens who meditate perched high on craggy trees. Even hummingbirds think more about life than I do. They are, after all, ancient warriors and the beloved of Left-Handed Hummingbird, the Aztec war god. They know life is about moving faster than the other guy.

No, I'm just a simple Jay. Or not so simple. After all, I've been hexed by a beleaguered Horned Owl. I was hazing her, swooping and calling her names (Flat-Face, Swivel Head, Gristle Up-Chucker). At first she cowered, being just a notch above a fledgling, but she was a strong one, more hooked into her mojo than I thought. Owls are wiser than mice, which isn't saying much. They do look smart with a ring of spectacle-like dark feathers around their big eyes. And they enjoy the dark hunt (the skitter of little paws in the leafy forest floor sends the blood pumping in their soulless hearts), but. But!

They have no sense of humor.

We Corvidae like a good joke. (Not directed toward us, of course.) We enjoy sitting on the scarecrow in the cornfield, waiting for the farmer to heave the hoe onto his shoulder and trudge back into his cornered nest. Maize is the food of this ancient land and part of our oral tradition.

We love (absolutely!) waking humans up at dawn with our Odes to Morning Defecating. Ravens sing about the Time of Famine and plucking out the eyeballs of dying soldiers. Magpies sing about strings of glittery threads and piles of buttons and bones. Jays sing about ourselves, our great shining beauty. Each jay may look similar to the human eye, which cannot see our *personal* auras. Mine is a midnight blue with sparks of fire and little twinkles of devil-may-care lime-green. It's natural for me to heckle owls and hawks, and I'm quite good at it.

This time, however, I was flummoxed to discover the Horned One was a regular Hecate. She sent the spell far-darting into my aura, my cloak of feathers, and deeper into my bones. She hexed and charmed, hawking up mangled bones with mouse ears (which she stirred with her claws into arcane symbols), clicked tonal variations of owl-mutter, and snapped her beak, cracking words into broken feathers. I shivered under her naked eyes (the whole dark moody moon look) and felt myself change, bones elongating, skull enlarging like a wasp nest, fingers growing where wing tips once fluttered.

She smirked and flew off into the cedars. I stood there, naked for several heartbeats, assessing my new body, flexing my muscles. I cocked my head and blinked. Two eyes, centered, was odd and a bit disorienting, but I soon got the hang of it.

My next step was to steal (snatch, borrow, scrounge) clothing. I wandered out of the forest, which was a finger of green stretching from the sea into the city. There was a street with rows of houses; it was curiously empty of people for the middle of the day. I saw shoes hanging up, laced together, over a long wire that stretched from one dead tree to another. I scratched my head. How could I get the shoes down without flying? I gave up, irritated at my new limitations. I hopped, and then modulated to a walk, into a backyard, where I found a blue jacket hanging on the back of a chair. I took it. It was a little big but OK. I loved the color.

Even then, I knew I needed more clothes. I saw how humans dressed. I had studied them, like all of my kind. It's a matter of survival. I needed pants and a shirt. I went into another yard. Nothing. A dog barked. I launched myself over the fence and ambled down the street. A bunch of my kin saw me, as they gathered around a bird feeder, and squawked, laughing. Tears suddenly rose in my eyes. I was alone, without my brethren or my sistren, and I didn't know how to be alone. I shook.

The air was summer-mild. I heard a human child shouting in the distance. One of those big machine birds flew overhead, loud and scary, the feathers decorated with a human head. Some of the geese and an eagle spread the rumor that humans are inside of those big birds, and maybe it is the Thunderbird spoken of so often in the Old Stories, the huge bird that ate people. But Raven said it was a machine that people made, a tool to let them fly like us. I wasn't sure of any of that then. Now, of course, I know what the human world is like. It is infinitely more devouring than Thunderbird.

I found pants, eventually, after scaring an old man when I appeared, naked, spitting out sunflower seeds from my pursed mouth. He backed away, his hands carrying a bucket of bird seed, and bumped into the house. He slumped down, eyes agog at my flying manhood (which curiously seemed to have a mind of its own at the oddest times). I cawed and when he closed his eyes (gone to roost in the middle of the day?), I stripped him. Dark blue pants in a heavy cloth, white bouncy shoes, a pale-breasted shirt that made me look like a bluebird (those namby-pamby meadow nitwits), and a hat that looked like a cow pie.

Later, I discovered he had a wallet in the pants pocket, with some money and cards with pictures of him. I went into the Lucky Market and bought a coffee. It was my first and tasted like worm juice. I spat it out and the woman screamed at me. I ran. I ran down the street and stopped to huff and gasp. There was a bench. I sat on it, next to a woman who inched herself away from me. A young man lounged against a pole. He pointed at me.

"You just sat on bird crap, man."

I understood his language, the intent of it but not the nuances. Was he saying I sat on a bird, crap-man? Was I ugly? (Oh, not to be borne!) The woman dug in her purse and offered me a white cloth. I looked at it.

"Well, do you want to wipe it off or not?" she asked. She motioned for me to stand up. "Here. You sat on it before I could warn you."

I stood up and tried to see my rear. I couldn't. I twisted this way and that. She sighed and told me to stand still.

Rolling her eyes, she turned to me. "I can't believe I'm doing this to a complete stranger, but if you want me to, I can wipe your butt."

I nodded. She made a few swipes with the cloth while the young man snickered.

"There," she said and got up to throw the cloth away in a metal can. "Ick! Why do they always crap on the bench? Last week, a gull almost got me!" She was round and plump as a dove, with an annoying nasal voice.

I spoke, my words slow and scratchy-sounding. "Gulls like to play games." They did, giving themselves points for on-target, shoulder-drop, and window-spatter.

She harrumphed, then peered at me. "Are you from this country? Excuse me for asking, but you have an accent."

"I am from here."

The young man looked up and pointed. "Bus coming." He added, "Guy's a little slow in the head." This time he pointed at me, twisting his finger by his ear.

The woman raised her eyebrows. "Everyone has his limitations, like some of us don't have a car. And some of us don't have any manners." She stared at him and then turned to me. "Are. You. Waiting. For. The. Bus?" She spoke like an inchworm.

"What is a bus?" I asked.

The young man gave me a look. "Seriously, dude?"

"A bus is serious?" I asked him, confused.

He laughed. "This dude is whack."

The woman glared at the young man. "Knock it off. Hey, if you want to know anything, go to the library." She opened her purse and dug out some shiny coins. "I used to be a librarian before I retired. The library holds the wisdom of the world."

The young man shrugged. "You're Old School. Go on the internet, man."

"Internet?"

The bus ground to a halt. The young man got on first. The woman said, "I'm going there now. Why don't you come with me?"

So I got on and paid from the old dude's wallet ("dude" is a term for mankind, I learned). I followed her down the aisle, sitting across from her. I was happy to be with a flock again.

A flock of one, not counting the dude with the spiky hair and the metal in his lips. He looked out the window.

I pointed at him, clearing my throat to get his attention. "Dude, I knew an eagle once got a fishing hook in his beak just like you. He starved to death. It was sad." I took a deep breath, tired from phrasing my thoughts.

His head reared back. "Dude! Don't dis my studs."

I frowned. I hadn't a clue as to his meaning.

I ended up going to the library every day. The old librarian was called Mary Jane. I told her my name was Jay Corvis. She taught me to read and said I picked it up faster than humanly possible, and she couldn't believe I was as slow as I seemed to be.

She canted her head. "You're smart, you know."

I nodded. "I come from a family of intelligent creatures."

She frowned. "But you don't talk like you've spoken to a lot of people, more like you learned to talk by reading . . . but you *just* learned to read. In a day!" She shook her head, amazed. I knew it was the Owl spell that had enchanted me.

She assumed I was homeless. Lots of homeless people sat in the library all day. Some of them smelled like cat pee. (Cats! Vile fangers! Sneaky snipers of claw!) Some of them were shape-shifters. I recognized a Great Raven, reading a graphic novel. One man had no legs. He walked like a bird on two thin stalks stuck into sneakers. I asked him if he was fowl or fauna and he taunted me, telling me he was the goat-god.

I found the soup kitchens and the long lines of dudes, nervously shuffling their feet. I slept in the woods. I stole more clothes from bins in parking lots (signs said *Drop off used clothing here*). I got used to being flockless, a loner like the northern shrike, that serial killer bird that impales voles on barbed fences (and enjoys watching them struggle). Not that I was a psycho like that, although I felt both dangerously fragile and unrestrained without the flock's collective will. I was constantly learning about *me* as an individual, and that was liberating.

The day I went into the library restroom was a major revelation. I saw how to pee after watching a dude stand, aim, and shake. But that wasn't the main astonishment. This was it: I saw myself in a mirror.

I was handsome. I had light brown skin and black hair. I had blue eyes. I was tall and strong-shouldered. Chicks looked at me, eyeing me with secret smiles.

Caw! Caw!

I read books about engines, cooking fowl (shudder), navigation, reflexology, astrology (I was a Pisces), Chinese history, fashion, and furniture making. I read mysteries, fantasy (not so unbelievable to me), and romance. I started flirting with the barista at the library coffee shop.

She was slender with blue eyes and hair the color of sunshine. We struck up a happy friendship based on my dislike of coffee (strangely enough, she hated coffee too) and my great thirst for mint tea (I tried varieties from seven different countries; Egyptian mint was my favorite). Her name was Skye.

Mary Jane, seeing I was such a quick study, hired me to do some genealogical research on her family. She paid me three days a week for four weeks. I was at the library a lot, looking into trees of human names and learning history, scanning lists and ledgers, trailing my finger down census forms, scribbling, jotting, scouring. I got enough money for food. I slept in the woods, near my old flock, who didn't recognize me, as far as I could tell. What happened to my beautiful aura, the aurora borealis of my soul?

I had been moping around the sci-fi paperback section one day when Skye appeared, turning the corner like a prism of light. Talk about auras! This young woman was flooding the air around her with waves of turquoise and magenta. Passion and the old blue jay team color.

"There you are," she said, smiling, handing me a cup of mint tea. The library, being very contemporary, allowed lidded drinks. "I saw you come in awhile ago. Why didn't you stop for your usual?"

I held on to the cup, which was burning from her hands (oh, joy!). I shrugged. "I don't know. I guess I'm out of sorts today."

We were very close. The aisles are wonderfully narrow when you want them to be, so that I could smell her rainbow-y scent and see the freckles on her cheeks. And those eyes! I could fly deep into them.

She touched my forearm. I felt the tingle all the way to my groin. She spoke quietly. "I missed seeing you, so I brought this to you myself on my break."

"Thank you," I whispered. The mint tea steamed between us.

She eyed me. "I like you, Jay." She spoke solemnly, but there was a tremor of . . . nervousness? . . . fear? . . . in her voice.

My throat was dry but I didn't dare sip the hot tea. I gulped. I'd read enough romance novels to understand what she was saying. But was she speaking from the old-school romance novels or the new, hot and heavy, nipples-at-attention books? What did "like" mean, exactly? I was picking at the words like a bird with a tough peanut shell.

Instead, I should've been more human and followed my instinct.

She waited. I cleared my throat. Then she lowered her hand and looked down.

"Okay," she said. "Well, I had to say what I was feeling, but it doesn't look like you feel that way, too, so forget it." She turned to go. Setting the cup down on the shelf, I touched her shoulder and stopped her.

"I like you, too," I said. "Very much."

"Oh!" She smiled. Then she darted a look. No one in sight. Sci-fi wasn't as popular as the mystery section. She stepped closer and lifted her face, waiting for the Kiss. (I knew the body clues from reading, but I'd never kissed a girl before, and blue jays don't have lips . . . of course! You know that . . . and I'd never even made love to a blue jay female, since I was hexed before I was old enough for the Spring Copulation. So I was stuck on the exact way to kiss.) I mean, do you close your eyes first (and risk missing the lips altogether?), or do you aim and place your lips on hers and then close your eyes? Blue jays have the courtship ritual down to specific moves: head bobble, body weave, beak touch, feather ruffle, tail lifting, approach and insert. I didn't think we could do that in the library.

So I just kissed her. Just went for it. Eyes wide open and then shut to feel the sensations of smooth lips, warm breath, moisture, heat, pulsation. I groaned and she sighed. It was just like a paragraph in a book, stopping short of the Next Step.

Skye suddenly jumped away. "Oh, my break's up!" She looked at me. "Jay, let's get together after work. Do you wanna do that?"

Finding my breath, I said sure. She left and I was dumbfounded. I'd kissed a human girl!

Now what? That was the Big Question. (And does "get together after work" mean *get together lustily,* or does it mean just going for a stroll down Hewitt Avenue?) Many questions lead up to the Big One.

Summer was almost over and I'd been feeling restless. It was the urge to flock, to be together for the long, hard winter, when food is scarce (if the humans forget to fill the feeders or if they're skinflints and don't put out beef suet cakes) and every blue jay is needed to alert the flock when food is around. We survived as a team, one big happy raucous, cantankerous family.

I was torn. I'd been sleeping in the woods, looking for that Witch Owl for weeks. Well, at first, I wanted to go back to being feathered. Lately, in spite of the Autumnal Congregation, I'd been less sure of what I'd been searching for.

Did I want to give up Skye for the sky? Did I want to become small and noisy and annoying to humans again, or did I want to be this good-looking chick magnet?

And how far could I go with Skye? All the way to heaven? Dude, I'd like to try that! But human girls are different. They don't automatically lift their tail feathers because nature must go on, reproducing itself forever. No, girls have choices.

In fact, being human meant choices and sometimes it was too confusing. Mint tea with honey or sugar? Soup line with sermon to follow or going hungry? War or peace? Spaghetti for dinner or fish? Newspaper or CNN? Paper or plastic?

I went to the Self-Help section and pulled out dozens of books, trying to find out how to make the right decision about anything. Trust your instinct. Don't trust it. Go with the flow. Use your head, not your heart. Make a list. Ask a friend to listen to you. Toss a coin. Read your daily horoscope. Make a wish on a falling star.

I decided to stay human. For the time being. Until I could find out what it was like to love a human female. I should be able to figure it out before winter.

By then, I'd know what it felt like to have sex (humans craved it, placed it up there above ice cream and breathing), and love would surely follow, or be in tandem with. Then, after I loved her, I would know the ultimate human experience, and I'd be okay with going back to my real self. I'd be just in time for winter stories told in the thickets of cedar and fir. I'd be able to tell the flock about what I did on my summer vacation. I'd understand what it meant to be human. I'd be looked up to as the Wise Jay, and come next spring, I'd have my pick of lovely young jaylings.

For love, human-style, must be brief. All stories come to an end. The last page of the novel is full of sighs, and we know they lived happily ever after—or else they seek that happiness with someone else. Humans don't mate for life like geese (those pompous, loyal speechifiers), and Skye will understand this, too. She won't mind my leaving; humans often fly solo.

Love and magic have one thing in common: transformation. Sometimes I think I've got it all figured out, and then my feathers prickle under my skin; my true nature has been turned inside out. I've been owl-hexed and girl-glamoured until my soul trembles in its nakedness. Maybe Skye wouldn't miss me if I left, but when I see her coming toward me with her arms outstretched and a smile on her lips, I feel like I'm stepping off a cliff, wingless.

THE SNOW QUEEN

In this wild country where winter is a keen blade, I found my shadow in the white wind. The snow blew and ice cracked on the bare branches of trees.

"Subject views herself as being followed by a shadow," whispered Dr. Andy Morton. He was seated next to Dr. Ellen Nighthorse, who leaned intently toward the glass window. On the other side, the patient, a woman named Joy B., was speaking to another doctor. The woman's dreamy voice captivated Dr. Nighthorse. It was smooth, gliding like skates on ice, with just enough of an edge to it to make you sit up and listen.

"When we stimulated the left temporoparietal junction of her brain, we discovered an interesting phenomenon. Her feelings of being followed by a shadow, of actually being *enveloped* by the shadow, were stimulated, too."

Dr. Nighthorse murmured, barely hearing Morton's scientific explanation. She was busy jotting down notes. Dr. Nighthorse was a psychologist; she was interested in the concept of a "shadow." Carl Jung stated that the shadow was the unconscious and repressed part in each of us. Everyone had a shadow, the dark aspects of our personalities. In Joy's initial statement she had mentioned finding and losing a shadow. Dr. Nighthorse couldn't wait to interview the patient herself.

The snow blew and that black night was my wedding night. I wore my best glacier gown, the one with snowflakes embroidered on it. I shivered as the dress slid over my shoulders, the snowflakes cold and glittering. My maid brushed out my long white hair and set the cap on my head. It was ice blue and sea green with a halo of white fox fur: my bridal tiara. I carried a bouquet of mistletoe.

I called down Siggurd, my familiar. He hooted from the tree outside. The maid opened the shutters at my command, letting in frigid air and a rush of snowy feathers. He sat on my shoulder, my right shoulder, so I could whisper to him in the old tongue. He clicked his beak. The maid cast nervous looks at me. I kept my face cold and regal.

"We were probing her brain with electrodes since we suspected she might have epilepsy." Dr. Morton glanced at the case papers. "When we found out her reaction to the stimulation, we realized how this might explain a lot of sensations people have. Like paranoia."

Dr. Nighthorse nodded.

"This case has become more complicated, as you can hear." Dr. Morton pointed at the patient. "She's talking about familiars . . . isn't that a term used by witches? She seems to think that she's some kind of queen, also. That's why we called you in."

At last, Dr. Nighthorse spoke.

"Yes, very interesting." She wanted to tell him to shut up so she could hear everything the patient was saying. It was being recorded but she wanted a first impression. The patient was a young woman, age twenty-nine, who called herself Freya. But her employee I.D. card said she was Joy Brown. She had been brought in to Emergency two weeks ago after a car jumped a curb and knocked her down as she was walking. She was the sole librarian at a private library maintained by eccentric millionaire H. Norman. His collection of rare books and mythology was little known by the general public. It was available for viewing by invitation only, and Dr. Nighthorse wondered how it could be a full-time job.

Ms. Brown had been admitted to the hospital while tests were being done. Mr. Norman had requested Dr. Nighthorse specifically. He'd told the police who contacted him later that he didn't know Ms. Brown very well. She did her job and their main contact was via e-mail or through his secretary.

The patient sat calmly in a cushioned chair, her arms resting on the table in front of her, hands clamped together. She had prematurely white hair, which cascaded down like a frozen waterfall over her shoulders. Her face was oval, with large blue eyes. She wore a long, blue cotton dress. She was slender, perhaps even graceful, although Dr. Nighthorse had not seen any significant movement. In fact, she didn't seem agitated or restless. She spoke directly to the doctor interviewing her, without any evasive body language.

Dr. Morton made a face. "Of course, nothing has explained her blue skin."

Dr. Nighthorse asked, "No history of using colloidal silver for dermatitis?"

100

"No." He tapped the folder. "And it's not a variation of Raynaud's Syndrome. Or a heart problem. We've gone through a lot of tests and theories, believe me. To be honest, we have no idea."

"What about her driver's license? Blue skin, too?"

"No driver's license."

"Huh. What does she say about it?"

Dr. Morton faced her directly. "She says it's the natural skin color of a queen." He rolled his eyes.

The wind blew and snow crystals sparkled in the air. We were wed in the Ice Palace. Candles made from caribou tallow flickered, reflected a hundredfold on the ice. The Court sat on robes spread over ice benches. Robes of ermine, fox, frost bear, and seal. Our realm is rich in luxurious furs; even the poor wear capes of snow rabbit. I stood facing the Court, head held high. I stomped on my bridal bouquet, for no other girl will wed for six months and a day. With my heel, I ground the white berries into the ice.

As we, the Royal Couple, passed down the aisle, the Court stood and bowed. The snow blew in through open windows, and Siggurd tucked his beak into the mass of my white tresses. We left the Ice Palace and entered ancient Myrkwood Castle, with its carved wooden eaves and immense posts hoisting the weight of the world.

In the Great Hall, tables had been laid with bowls of salted herring, platters of seal fat and smoked eel, saucers of cloud berries, pots of caribou butter, and salads of seaweed and roe. Delicacies from the Far South were spread out among the guests: apples, honeyed walnuts, baked turnips, lamb, and candied rose hips. We nibbled a bit and then left them to their merriment. Hand in hand, my husband and I ascended the stairs.

Our wedding chamber was warm. Siggurd flew to his perch and turned his back to us. My husband faced me, a slight sheen to his white skin. The fire crackled and snow blew down the chimney, hissing in the flames. The wide-planked wood floors were bleached and rubbed to a soft finish. My slippers, worn only this once, glided on the floor as I neared him. My hand touched his cheek, while his hand tilted my chin up. We kissed and the heat made my lips burn.

Our bed was a snowy field, the coverlet made of white southern cotton and stuffed with eiderdown. My husband, Hjalmar Magnussen, was tall with hair the color of the full moon. He unbuttoned my dress and gently pulled it off over my shoulders, past my breasts, and then with an impatient tug over my hips. It fell in a melted puddle at my feet. I stepped over it and undid the laces of his shirt, teasing the material down his broad shoulders.

Soon we stood naked, hands at our sides. We stared, taking full measure of each other. We devoured our beauty, our curves and muscles, our tendons and soft hairs, our hollows and rises.

We folded back the coverlet and climbed in. Pulling it over our heads, we made a cave like two silly children. But what we did next was not childish.

"Stop." Dr. Nighthorse rose and pushed the intercom button. On the other side of the window, the doctor half-turned in her chair and faced the glass, eyebrow raised. "That's enough for now."

The interviewer nodded and gathered her tape recorder, turned off the camera, and stood up. She motioned with her hands for Ms. Brown to rise and precede her out the door.

The patient sat with a puzzled look on her face. Finally, she stood up, slowly pushing herself to her feet. She turned toward the window and mouthed, "Who?" or perhaps she only blew air from her blue lips.

The next day, Dr. Nighthorse sat with her in her room. It was a pleasant room with a brightly colored bedspread and a desk with a hot pink blotter. The sun streamed through the windows, through the bars of steel mesh that made melted-cube-like shadows on the floor. There were two chairs meant to suggest visitors and friendly talks. There was a supply of paper and pens, a wall lamp with a pale blue shade. It was a room to cheer up a patient, subtly lifting the mood by color and texture.

Ms. Brown sat in a white robe, hospital issue, and paper slippers. Her hands were on her knees.

"Are you going to help me?" she asked.

"I hope so." Dr. Nighthorse nodded. "Let's talk about what you need."

With a note of exasperation in her voice, the patient replied, "I need for you to break the spell!"

"What spell?"

"Don't be stupid!" Joy crossed her arms. "I will not have it!"

The doctor tilted her head. "Joy, I don't understand. Please tell me exactly what you mean."

"Don't call me Joy. My name is Freya."

"It says on your identity card that your name is Joy Brown."

"I don't know what you're talking about."

Dr. Nighthorse pulled out a photocopy of an employee card for Norman, Inc. "Look."

Joy took the paper and eyed it. "I don't know who that is."

"It has your photo on it," the doctor pointed out.

Joy shrugged. "It looks like me, but I am not Joy Brown."

"All right. Then let me try to understand. You want me to call you Freya. You are a queen and you got married recently." At the patient's nod, the doctor went on. "And by our records your name is Joy Brown. You work as a librarian for a private library. You are twenty-nine years old, 5'11". You live in an apartment at the library."

Joy shook her head. "No. No. That's all wrong. I live in Myrkwood Palace in the Far North."

"The far north from where?"

Joy stared at her. "From where?"

The doctor nodded. "Like, in Canada? Or Europe? I notice you have a slight accent. In fact, I must point out that you speak English."

Joy frowned. "It is the Far North. It is not anywhere else. I don't understand these other places you mention. I don't know why I speak your tongue, but I do. It's the enchantment. The spell must be broken, or I will never return." She stood up and faced the window. "The only thing that matters to me is Hjalmar. I want my husband back. I want his shadow."

"Tell me about it."

When the six months and one day passed, still I was not with child, even though the sun came and the light grew. The snow steamed over the brooks, blue ice dribbled down the rocky cliffs, pastures became soggy with cold runoff. The wind blew and my husband cradled my hips. He entered me and the sun shone on his back so that all of his fine hair gleamed like gold. We lay under the green-black trees or out in the blooming meadows. We ate the sun, chewing it slowly, letting the warmth enter our bellies. We listened to the herders' echoing songs. We lay in each other's arms and felt blessed. Hjalmar was a good man, but I did not become gravid.

My sister, Gertha, followed him one day. She opened her robe to him, and he saw her nakedness. But he did not go to her. The people said there must be a child, and if I could not provide, then she must. But he would not lie with her.

So she took his shadow.

And I have not seen him since.

Dr. Nighthorse was deep in thought. Joy/Freya sat on the edge of her bed, quiet, with a faraway look in her eyes.

Jung suggested that "the psychological rule says that when an inner situation is not made conscious, it happens outside as fate." So what was Joy's situation?

What was the truth to her story? On the surface, it looked like she was sad because she hadn't been able to get pregnant. But there were other details that made the case interesting: a fantasy world, a (fantasy?) husband, a sister who wanted to seduce her husband, a sister who stole him. And the blue skin.

Somehow it was going to be Dr. Nighthorse's job to make all this clear, not only to herself but to the patient.

We all have our secrets, sometimes even to ourselves. The doctor knew that. And the idea of a "sister" was often just a variation of the Shadow, another part of our self. And what did she mean by her husband's shadow being stolen by the rejected seductive sister? Did she herself feel rejected? Or did her husband actually leave her when she didn't get pregnant?

"Tell me more about your sister and your husband."

Gertha collects frogs and eats them. She wears a belt that is blood-red. She has hair that twists like dusky roots. Her voice is harsh and she sneered at me when I announced my engagement to Hjalmar.

But I was the chosen, by birthright and by the stars.

Even so, I loved her. She is my little sister.

I loved her the way you care for a spindly calf, who has a great fire to live but is sickly.

She has a soul sickness and spends the long nights studying the darkest of spells.

She grew more beautiful as she got older. Whether it is the spells or some kind of natural beauty, I don't know. My looks, however, have faded since I lost my husband.

Our life is spent in six moons of night and six of day. We rejoice when the sun never sets, and the women shake out their skirts and smile boldly at the men. The men stomp their boots and stand up straighter, free from the burden of snow.

Hjalmar loved me. I know this. It was not because he must mate with me but because he loved me for myself.

That she took him away from me is something I will never forgive. She took his shadow and now he is gone.

Notes from Dr. Nighthorse: I asked her to tell me what taking a shadow meant, and she looked at me oddly. "Don't you know what a shadow is?" she asked me. I pointed to her shadow patterning the floor. She said she didn't see it. I traced the outline with my fingertip, and she shook her head. She said her shadow always *follows* her; it is never stationary or attached to her. Gradually, I began to understand that she thinks her shadow is an active entity, something that follows her constantly and has a mind of its own. She said that the shadow hates being cooped up in the hospital. She feels unattached to her own feelings, alienated from her inner self.

From this, I gathered that her subconscious self is her shadow, talking to her and allowing her to speak about issues she would rather repress. She feels enveloped by this shadow because it is outside of her normal awareness.

When I asked her to explain her husband's shadow, she said it was his essence. This added another element to the situation. Apparently, the shadow is a soul concept to her. But I didn't understand a soul that also had its own opinions.

"Did your husband physically disappear?" I asked her, and she said that when the shadow is gone, so is the person. Which is more real to her: her actual husband or his shadow/soul concept? Or did he ever exist at all?

I looked up "Freya" on the internet. As I skimmed the material, I gasped. Freya, a Scandinavian goddess, had a husband who disappeared!

So, Joy must be well versed in mythology. She modeled her life on an ancient myth. Or her husband really disappeared and she adapted the myth to suit her circumstances.

I'm still trying to unravel the complexities of this case.

Addendum: Ms. Brown's employer, Mr. Norman, sent me a letter suggesting that she be released into his care. Because she is not legally committed here, I've explained to her that she can do this if she wishes. He's asked that I continue working with the patient. Staff will be available to cook and clean for her in her apartment. It sounds like a good idea. She'll be in familiar surroundings, and perhaps that will let her be more relaxed.

The library was in an old mansion built by a lumber baron a century ago. It was a warren of rooms. Dr. Nighthorse passed by a door with a plaque that announced the Norman Library was open only by appointment. A quiet woman led her up a curving stairway, down a long hall that turned at several angles, to a suite overlooking the rear garden. When she knocked, the patient opened the door. A blast of cool air billowed out. The servant left and Dr. Nighthorse entered the room.

Joy looked vibrant. Her movements were quick, her long, flowered dress swirling around her ankles.

"Isn't this wonderful?" she asked, smiling. "The air is so fresh!"

The doctor shivered slightly, glad she'd worn a light sweater. "It seems cool."

"Of course! It is like the Far North." She closed her eyes briefly. When she opened them, she looked directly at the doctor.

"You always ask me questions, but I don't know anything about you. I don't understand your name. Nighthorse? What does this mean?"

"I'm a doctor who wants to help you. We've talked about that before. My last name is from my Native American heritage. It was given to my great-grandfather in a vision. It was said that he saw a horse racing across the night sky, stars streaming from its tail. I think it was an old-fashioned way of describing a comet."

Joy snorted. "Or perhaps it was just exactly what he said it was."

The doctor bit her lip and didn't answer. How could she explain that she was a modern Native woman, proud of her tradition but living in the here and now? Everything had a reasonable explanation if you were willing to dig hard enough.

Joy led her over to a sitting area that was part of a Victorian turret. Windows curved above pillowed benches. Outside a huge old maple spread its branches. Tea, a pot of strawberry jam, toast, and a bowl of fruit were on a small round table. They sat and were soon busy spreading jam and pouring tea.

"I didn't know you had such luxuries here," Joy said around a mouthful of toast. "You live like royalty!" She sounded like she'd never eaten jam before.

"Anyone can buy this food in a store."

"This is a strange land. The cook tells me he's never eaten caribou!" She shook her head in disbelief.

"Have you spoken with your boss yet?" The doctor had been trying to make an appointment with him, but his secretary said he was too busy.

"No."

"I'd like to talk to him."

Joy studied her. "You want to talk about me, don't you?"

The doctor nodded. "Maybe he can give me some input on your past. He must've looked into your previous work history and references when he hired you."

"I've told you before that I don't even remember him or being here before. I know nothing except waking up in the hospital." Joy wiped her mouth with a pale green linen napkin. "You know, there are tales of our people being lured into Summerland and never coming back. It's said that they are seduced by the food and the sensual delights. I must say that the food here is better than at the hospital, and I can almost understand why someone would want to stay here. But," she sighed, "I want to go home."

"This apartment is your home."

"No! Don't be obtuse! I am talking about my queendom! Your world is magical with its wheels and noises, the tall stone buildings, the small talking boxes, and flowers blooming. Your land is like the old fairy tales where one partakes of the food and falls into a deep dream." She trembled. "But I will go back! No amount of magic will keep me from my home."

"This is reality, Joy, not a made-up world. We're not fairies. There's no magic involved in how cars run or what you can buy in the store. You've created your own world to avoid facing problems in this one."

Joy stared at the doctor. She dropped her butter knife on the plate with a clatter. "You're trying to deceive me!" She looked around, her eyes darting. "All of this is to distract me from seeking my husband! I know that!" She took a deep breath and spoke more calmly. "I know that. Your enchantment is cruel and cunning." She bent her head. "I only want to find my husband." She put her face in her hands.

The doctor was quiet for a moment. Then she said, "Joy, we've gone over and over the realities of your life as we know it. There are some mysteries. We don't know why your skin is blue. We don't have any record of you before last year when you started working for Norman. No driver's license or Social Security card. Perhaps you're an illegal. Or trying to escape an abusive relationship. But whatever it is that you're running from, please believe me when I say that I'm not deceiving you or trying to trick you in any way. I want to help you, Joy."

The woman stood, her fists clenched at her sides.

"I will not speak to you unless you address me by my name. I am Freya the Snow Queen." She narrowed her eyes.

For the rest of the session, she wouldn't speak to Dr. Nighthorse. That night, the doctor called her mentor, Dr. John Muller.

After a long discussion, she decided to call Joy by her fantasy name. Although she hadn't wanted to reinforce or buy into Joy's fantasy, John said nothing would be gained by silence.

"Explain to the patient that you will call her Freya but that you still think she's Joy. That way, she'll see the boundaries you've set, and she'll talk to you."

"But won't that give her power to set those boundaries?"

"Perhaps, but what are we really talking about here, Ellen? Boundaries for what? Her fantasy world? *You* know it's fantasy and that's what really matters."

"Please call me Ellen and I'll agree to call you Freya," began the doctor, wincing a bit as she said it. "I'm really fascinated and curious about your blue skin."

Freya shrugged listlessly. "My skin is blue. What more can I say?"

"But no one else has blue skin."

"No, of course not."

Puzzled, Ellen frowned. "Explain."

Freya looked annoyed. "Only the Snow Queen has blue skin. It is an ancient custom."

"How can skin color be a custom?"

Freya shrugged again. "When my engagement was announced, it was done."

"By magic?'

She raised her chin. "You really don't know anything, do you?" She shook her head. "Some things are not talked about." And she wouldn't elaborate.

Ellen knew her patient was blue all over, even her scalp was blue. It had been in the original medical report. Confused, she tried a different tack.

"How long ago were you married? You've been a little vague on this."

Freya sat on the window seat, legs curled to one side. She wore her hair in a braided coronet. Her dark emerald-colored dress was tucked under her ankles. She leaned her head against the window. Her skin, lightly tinged with blue, shone in the reflected golden glow of autumn maple leaves. It gave her skin a slightly greenish cast, like verdigris, that greenish patina of weathered copper.

"Ages ago." Freya was quiet, even hesitant.

"Can you be more precise?"

"I was much younger then."

The doctor waited, hoping Freya would continue, but she remained close-mouthed.

"Are you feeling sick today, Freya?"

The woman shook her head. "I am well but full of sorrow. I miss my Siggurd, also. It's been so long."

"Tell me about Siggurd."

I cannot explain him exactly. I have no words. But he is linked to my soul and beautiful. His feathers are white with tufts of down by his ears. His eyes are dark and knowing. He was torn from me when I was hurled to this void, your world, and I doubt that he lives now.

I raised him from an egg. His mother was killed by a falcon, and I took the eggs and gave one to Gertha. Her egg rotted. She was furious and she threw it at me.

We have always been at war, it seems. I gave her a caribou, and it died from worms in its stomach. I gave her a length of fine wool, and the moths ate it. I gave her the gold cup our father left to us, and she melted it down to make a collar for her raven, Kjrk. And then she complained that she had no jewels. She said that everything I had was better than what she possessed. And worse, she believed I had cursed her when she was a baby.

108

Gertha hated Siggurd. He kept a careful eye on her. Siggurd knew that it was Gertha's falcon that killed his mother. He told me this and I held him close. His small body shook with sorrow and anger. Gertha truly killed him by casting me out, and she took my husband, so that she killed three. Now I am sure that she rules in my place.

The Far North was changing even before I was spirited away. The frost bears were dying. The ice was melting earlier, and the glaciers shrinking. The caribou were sickening. I was told to bear a child, a true child of the Far North, one who would bring back the pure cold. But I failed.

Yes, the ice rots and the snow drizzles, the wind blows yellow dust, and the furry ones die shrunken and starved on the tundra. It is my fault. I'm barren. The Ice Castle decays, melting more each warm season. Once Hjalmar and I stood so proud and hopeful!

Now all is gone.

She stopped speaking suddenly, head down. The doctor frowned. This fantasy was taking on epic proportions. Now global warming was part of it. The patient was getting worse, wrapping layer upon layer around her persona, developing more ways to cushion herself against reality. She even looked ill, her face drawn and the white hair lank. Ellen could swear that she was less blue than before. Yes, she was definitely paler, her lips thin and chapped.

"Freya, I can't find any society that believes the way you do. Not the Danes, Swedes, Norwegians. Not the Icelandic or the Sami people. I mean, everyone knows the old stories about Freya, but that's all they are. Old stories. No one *lives* in the world you described." Ellen paused, suddenly getting an idea. "Instead of my asking you about your world, why don't I show you the one you're living in now?"

Freya looked up. "What do you mean?"

"Let's go out! You already know what its like to sit in a car, but how about if we go for a ride and stop at a store or a park?" Ellen was excited. Maybe she could integrate both worlds.

"I don't know." Freya bit her lip. "It's frightening out there. So strange." She pointed to the window.

"It's strange only because you aren't interacting with the world. You've put yourself outside of it and separate from it. I think we should start with a simple walk around the neighborhood."

Freya wrapped her arms around herself. "Let me think about it."

The doctor had to be content with that for the moment.

When she got home from her session with Joy, Ellen found a message on her phone. She was to meet with Mr. Norman tomorrow at ten o'clock sharp.

So the next morning she drove back to the mansion. Apparently, Norman lived in the south wing. Ellen fumed. He'd been so close all along! Well, she knew he was reported to be almost a hermit. The rich eccentrics, she told herself, are not the happiest people in the world.

She was shown in to the formal lobby and then escorted down a long hallway to a double door. It had an intercom next to it. The servant pushed the button, spoke a few words, and the door clicked open. Ellen was a little unnerved when the servant gestured her in by herself. The door shut behind her.

Her footsteps echoed down a marble hallway. Closed doors lined the hall, and she was confused. She stopped and wondered what to do. Then a door opened and a woman stepped out.

She beckoned to Ellen, turned around, and went back into the room.

Ellen raised her eyebrows. Rude. But she followed the woman and entered a small office. The woman sat behind a rosewood desk. A computer sat on top, along with a stack of mail, papers, and a globe with a snow scene. A plastic white rose stood up stiffly in a rather ugly white vase.

The woman was odd. Her lashes had to be fake. They were thick and crusted with black mascara. Her skin was too pale, the foundation just not right for her. Her dark hair was crinkly and held back by a big, retro black headband. But she was beautiful. Her lips were full and reddened by the perfect lip gloss color. Her cheekbones were sculpted. Her eyebrows arched over blue eyes.

Her voice was nasal and a bit of a shock. Ellen expected something more professional or cultured.

"Mr. Norman will see you in a moment. Would you like some coffee?"

"No, thanks." Ellen looked around. The room was a mixture of Danish furniture and sixties décor: a sleek coffee table and sofa under a poster with a colorful peace sign. A Rubik's Cube was perched on the table alongside a graceful and spotless ashtray. Somehow the room and the woman matched.

"Mr. Norman doesn't usually grant interviews. You may have heard that he is reclusive." When Ellen nodded, the secretary went on. "I'm his personal assistant. My name is Jennifer Smith." She reached into a desk drawer and pulled out a box. It held a supply of mouth masks. She took two out. "Mr. Norman is a germophobe. I don't know if that's the proper medical term for it"— she gave a small chuckle—"but we have to wear these." A soft chime sounded from the intercom on her desk. "Oh, that's our cue. Please come this way."

The secretary handed a mask to Ellen, who looked at it for a moment and then gave a mental shrug. She looped the strings over her ears and patted the mask into place. Ms. Smith nodded as she donned her own mask.

110

Ellen followed her into a huge room. It was an obvious addition to the mansion, because it had large, floor-to-ceiling windows. But they were covered up with navy curtains. The chilly room felt claustrophobic even though it was spacious. A large desk was placed opposite a cold fireplace. The desk was completely bare. There was no computer, either. Bookcases lined the walls, however, and were so crammed that books spilled over onto the floor. Small table lamps dotted the gloom with tiny circles of light.

In front of the desk were two chairs. They were placed about six feet from the desk. A man stood stiffly behind the desk.

He wore a mask over his mouth. His eyes were weary, the skin sagging underneath. His hair was thinning and gray. His skin was pasty white. He looked like a sick man. Maybe that's why he didn't like to meet people, Ellen thought. Maybe he was afraid of germs because he had a compromised immune system.

"He won't shake hands with you," said the secretary. "Please take a seat." She motioned toward a chair. Ellen sat down but felt awkward. He was about eight feet away. She was disconcerted to see the secretary sit down in the other chair.

"How do you do, Mr. Norman," she said in a raised voice. "My name is Dr. Nighthorse. I'd like to speak to you about Joy Brown, your librarian." She glanced at Ms. Smith. "And I'd like to speak in private. I'm sure you'll appreciate that confidentiality is . . ."

Ms. Smith interrupted. "I stay. Mr. Norman needs me."

"But . . ."

There was a moment of silence. Mr. Norman sat down. Ellen frowned.

"OK. Well, I'm not at liberty to overstep patient confidences, but I can say that Ms. Brown needs a lot more therapy. I'd like any background info you can give me that will be helpful."

"There's nothing we can add," said the secretary.

Ellen ignored her and spoke directly to Norman. "Sir?"

He ran his hand over his eyes. He cleared his throat and then looked at his assistant.

She spoke. "Mr. Norman doesn't like to talk."

Exasperated, Ellen clenched her fists as she leaned forward. "Then why did you agree to see me? Really, I need . . ."

"You don't need anything more, doctor. Mr. Norman agreed to see you because you were so persistent, even to the point of harassment." Ellen's mouth fell open. Before she could protest, the secretary went on in her irritating voice. "He wishes to assure you that you will be paid, however . . . your services are no longer required."

"What!" Ellen's gaze bounced back and forth between the two people. Ms. Smith's voice was coldly severe, as if she were enjoying her power and role as spokesperson. Mr. Norman had an air of distraction, and Ellen suddenly wondered if he had Alzheimer's.

"Mr. Norman wants me to inform you that Ms. Brown has been removed to a private hospital."

Ellen sputtered. "Why?"

"She went into a catatonic state last night. For her own good she needs twenty-four-hour care."

"Where is she? I'll continue my work with her there."

The woman shook her head. "No, we prefer to use the in-house doctors. I have a check ready. I've added a substantial sum, since we had to abort your sessions earlier than expected." She rose.

Ellen stayed seated. "Mr. Norman, this is highly irregular. I'd like to hear what you have to say." She waited. "From your own lips." His assistant gave a nod.

Behind the mask, his voice was gravelly and slightly sarcastic. "Ms. Smith knows best." He gave a little nod and focused on the doctor. There was a pleading look in his eyes. Suddenly, he groaned and rubbed his temple. "Excuse me, I've had a terrible headache all day. I'm not used to visitors, and I've been anxious about our visit." He placed his hands on the desk and leaned forward. "I trust Ms. Smith to take care of everything." His voice was muffled behind the mask, but she heard him clearly.

"Mr. Norman," said the secretary in a low voice. "Please don't distress yourself. We're leaving." She waited by Ellen's chair. After a moment, Ellen rose, uncertain but not able to think of anything else to say or do.

In the outer room, the secretary took off her mask and went to her desk. She opened a drawer and took out a check. She handed it to Ellen, who took it reluctantly after removing her mask.

"I trust you will find this sufficient." She led the way to the door. "Please don't worry about Joy. She is receiving the best of care."

"I, er, I left a nice pen in her room. I'd like to go look for it."

"Really?" Ms. Smith's eyes were cool. "I shall ask the staff. Her room has been cleaned. Nothing remains."

"But . . . surely, you expect . . . you hope Joy will recover? I'd really like to speak to the doctor."

She shook her head. "It doesn't look promising. Listen, I can tell you that Joy was a troubled woman when she came to work for Mr. Norman." She lowered her voice, glancing back toward his office. "She seemed a little . . . off balance, I suppose you'd say . . . and a loner. I assumed librarians were like that, you know, enjoying books more than real people. But she developed a crush, or maybe an obsession, on Mr. Norman. He found it extremely uncomfortable, even distasteful. He chose to limit his contact with her."

"Why didn't anyone tell me this before? It's important!" Ellen gritted her teeth.

Ms. Smith shrugged. "It doesn't matter now. I'm only telling you that Joy was the kind of person to fantasize. She once told me to call her Mrs. Norman!" She shook her head. "Maybe she had me fooled. Maybe she was just a mousy gold digger, after his money. But she was creepy. I didn't like her. After the accident, she got worse. Whenever I talked to her, she retreated into her own little world."

"You talked to Joy?"

She nodded. "I came to visit her every day, to see how she was doing, make sure she had enough to wear, you know . . . just see if she needed anything. She asked for only one thing."

"What?"

"A toy owl. I got one of those Harry Potter owls, you know, the white ones. She insisted it was real." Ms. Smith crossed her arms. "Perhaps I should've told you about that, but I didn't see any harm."

Ellen was livid. She spoke carefully. "It might have helped if you told me what was going on."

"Well, that's water under the bridge now, isn't it?" Ms. Smith lifted one arm to direct Ellen down the hallway.

Ellen paused. "And tell me, Ms. Smith, did you draw any conclusions about her blue skin?"

Ms. Smith blinked. "I wouldn't call it 'blue' exactly. More like gray. I was told it was due to her being anemic."

"No, she wasn't anemic. Her skin was definitely bluish."

Ms. Smith shrugged. "I don't think it looked blue, but . . ." Her voice trailed off. She gestured again and Ellen had to follow her.

As she walked, she wished she could inspect Joy's room, but she wasn't given a chance. Ms. Smith went with her all the way to the front door.

As the door closed behind her, Ellen stood on the wide porch, purse in one hand, check in the other, and sighed.

That afternoon, she was at her desk organizing her notes on the case when she got a phone call. It was from Dr. Morton, Andy. She was on a first-name basis with him, having gone out for coffee one day and lunch another. She liked him. He was funny and smart. Not really handsome but not unattractive.

"Woad," he said.

She was confused. "Woad what?"

"Woad, you wittle wabbit."

"Andy! What the heck are you talking about?" she said, laughing.

"It was woad. The skin dye for your patient Joy Brown." He went on to explain that the skin sample they'd sent to the lab revealed woad, a natural plant dye.

"Woad, huh. That's amazing. I can't . . ." Ellen paused, thoroughly baffled. "OK. So she dyed her skin. Every inch of it. How is that even possible?"

"I dunno. Probably immersed herself in a tub of blue dye."

"But why?"

"I dunno. That's your department." He chuckled. "Why don't you just ask your Smurfette?"

"Because she's not my patient anymore." She explained what had happened earlier that day.

"Gee, that's too bad. Hey, before I get back to work, I want to ask you if you want to go out for dinner tomorrow night."

After they arranged the details, they hung up. Ellen tapped her pen on the desk. She'd asked her secretary, Ashley, to call around the local hospitals and clinics earlier, but there was no record of Joy Brown. It didn't seem like a crime had been committed, but it was a mystery. Where was Joy Brown? Was she OK?

Just before she left to go home for the day, Ashley brought in a fax. It was from a Dr. Hirshfield, who was notifying her, as professional courtesy, that Joy had died. Apparently, she had been not catatonic but in a coma. She'd been advised that Dr. Nighthorse had been working with the deceased and thought she'd like to know. Joy Brown was to be cremated. There would be no memorial service, since no one could locate family. If Dr. Nighthorse wanted to speak to Dr. Hirshfield, she could call the following number.

She picked up the phone and dialed immediately. A recorded voice told her that Dr. Hirshfield was not available at this time. She left a message and her phone number.

Ellen sat, trembling. She thought for a long time before she called the police. She spoke with a woman who took down her concerns and promised to get back to her.

The next day, Ellen tried to call Dr. Hirshfield again. She was still unavailable. She called the police and spoke with the desk sergeant. He told her he'd call her back.

She had dinner with Andy and told him everything. He didn't have any words of wisdom, but it was good for her to have someone to talk to.

She spent an awful lot of time listening attentively to others' problems.

Finally, two days later, the police called. They had a death certificate signed by Dr. Hirshfield, a doctor well known in Arcadia, Washington. The Arcadian police had verified the existence of the Wellspring Clinic, and it was legit.

Dr. Hirshfield never called her back. There was always a recorded message. Eventually, Ellen gave up. The case was filed away, and, if not forgotten, it was nonetheless concluded.

She never remembered dreaming about two sisters, one with light hair and one with dark, facing each other in a shadowy dance of hate and love. Two sisters in love with the same man.

She did go back to the mansion a month later. She was determined to talk to someone about Joy. But the mansion was boarded up. A sign posted on the door said that it was closed for remodeling.

Ellen wandered around the grounds. A late autumn wind was gusting, and she pulled her scarf closer around her throat. She hurried around the corners of the building, trying to find Joy's room on the third floor. She searched for the old maple. There were several but she found the one she wanted immediately. A stuffed owl was perched forlornly on a bare branch.

Was this Siggurd? Or to be more accurate, the genesis for the idea of a familiar?

There were many unanswered questions. Ellen left, feeling sad and dissatisfied. She wanted closure, that sense that all the loose ends were tied up. She knew that life wasn't like that. She drove away and went to meet Andy for lunch.

Gertha watched Ellen drive off. She let the curtain fall back and turned toward him. He was sitting by the unlit fireplace. A floor lamp glowed weakly in one corner, and the room was full of shadows.

He had a warm blanket wrapped around his legs. He wore a gray sweater and flannel pants, and had a cup of cold tea in one hand. The other hand lay limply on his lap. A pile of books were on the floor by his feet.

She took off her headband and glasses, and rubbed off the heavy foundation with a tissue. "Good bye, Ms. Smith," she mumbled under her breath. It had been a lot of work to change her appearance every day. She shook out her dark hair. She had a hard time thinking of herself as a "Jennifer." It had irritated her to be addressed by such an ordinary, rather common, name.

"The doctor's gone. She looked like she'd lost her best friend." Gertha clucked her tongue. "I must say that she served her purpose." Everyone knew that Joy Brown had been crazy, especially after the doctor voiced her concerns to the police. Now it was on record that Joy was mentally unbalanced. And dead.

She went over and knelt in front of him. She took the cup and placed it on a table. Then she took both of his hands in hers. "I want you to sign the papers today. Can you do that for me?"

He looked at her blankly and then nodded. "It's time?"

"Yes, it's getting darker and darker. Haven't you noticed?"

He frowned. "I thought it was just me." He rubbed his eyes.

She smoothed down his hair. It was wispy and gray, so unlike the thick mane of his youth. Never mind. He may have lost vitality and manly vigor since then, but he was still worth a lot. Soon it would be hers. He just needed to sign the papers. It would all work out.

She'd always wanted him, even when he chose that bitch over her. Well, she was gone now and good riddance. He made love to that white-haired loony, and Gertha had almost died from jealousy. The pain was still there under her breastbone, like a raven pecking at her heart.

Gertha would restore his health. It just would take time. At least, she hoped he hadn't been constrained too long. She was sure that a few weeks in the cold mountain air would cure him. A good diet, off his meds, and he'd be his old self. She longed to touch him and to feel his strength inside of her.

He would forget *her,* that woman who always seemed to have everything going her way. Gertha nearly spit. How she had laughed to name her adversary "Joy"; it was rich, wasn't it? Once it had been her childhood nickname. It had made Gertha gag when she heard people say, "Oh what a joy that girl is!" Well, now who was laughing? The irony!

Gertha smiled to herself.

She got up and went to her briefcase. She reached in and brought out two papers. Grabbing a pen, she carried it all over to him. "Look, here they are. Just sign here and here," she said, flipping over a page to show him.

"Sign?"

"That's right. Sign here." She jabbed a finger on a dotted line. "We talked about this yesterday. It's for your kingdom."

"My kingdom."

She nodded. "Remember the Far North and the kingdom of ice? Remember the stories I told you? How you'd be healthy and happy there?"

"Stories?"

"Memories. I meant to say memories." She made her voice calm and loving. "You know how much you miss it. If you sign, then we can go there." Gertha forced herself to be patient. She could hardly wait to assume control of all the riches!

"But where's my queen?" He frowned and looked around as if he could find her in the shadows.

"She's gone, dead now for a very long time," Gertha said gently.

"Really?" He paused, gazing into space. "It seems like just yesterday."

She shook her head. "Trust me. It was long ago. And the kingdom needs a new queen. Once the old one is gone, there needs to be a new one. You understand that."

He nodded. "Or else the world will die. All the snow will melt and the waters rise. And, lo, the land shall be inundated. The vast herds of caribou shall vanish, and the mountains of ice shall crumble into the void of the sea," he intoned.

"That's right. That's exactly right." She jiggled the pen to get his attention. He blinked and looked at it. Taking it up, he paused.

"But my queen shall have the blue mark upon her."

"I do, my king. Look." She lifted her hands and he focused, blinking rapidly again. "And look." She turned her face toward his. He peered at her. She hoped it was blue enough for him to see in the dim room. She'd spent hours studying ancient tomes for the right potion, and months putting her plan into action. It hadn't been easy getting all the ingredients. She tapped a blue finger on the page.

"Ah." He smiled, putting pen to paper. It was a sweet smile, one of remembered joy.

THE VAMPIRE AND THE
MOTH WOMAN

DEDICATED TO BARBARA CARRICO

The first time I saw the vampire, I was feeding from a rhododendron blossom, its red petals dark in the night. He stopped, searching for my presence, and listened with his uncanny hearing. My tiny heart beat too loud, too fast. His eyes widened as he found me. Moving swiftly, he pounced, cupping me in his hands. I trembled, caught in a fleshy cave that smelled of blood salts and desiccated skin. He lifted one hand to peer at me as I stood in the center of his palm, antennae quivering.

When he exhaled, the rush of air reminded me of old meat, mold, and roots. It was a rich smell, reminiscent of larvae and the thick leafy underworld of the forest.

"What thing are you?" he whispered. I heard him through my hearing organs on each side of my thorax.

I was afraid. I released scents, hormonal communication, even though I could've spoken through the long tube of my proboscis. All moth shape-changers are female. I don't know why. I seldom saw other moth women, because there are so few of us. Because we are born human, we retain human thoughts and speech. And yet we are not completely human. Our shape changing occurs when the sun abandons us to night and wings and the terror of insect-eating bats. I'd had a few close calls with bats, but I never thought I'd see its notorious sidekick, a vampire. I didn't even believe in vampires.

Yet I instantly understood what he was. He wore a black T-shirt and dark pants. He was barefoot. His face was pale, lean with high cheekbones, and eyes black as a spider's heart. His hair was the color of wet cedar bark.

He turned his palm, observing me. "You're not pretty. Brown and gray." I had a delicate white ruffle along my wings that I was proud of, but I knew I wasn't beautiful. "Your body is fat, like a grub. Yet you are exquisite, a being of the night like me. I don't understand what you are. I sense human feelings of fear and loathing." He talked softly.

Suddenly, he made a fist and I was trapped. I heard him through his hollow bones.

"I could kill you. I could crush you and throw you down. Grind you under my heel." Then he opened his hand and I spread my wings. "But I won't. Go!"

I flew toward my house. Leaves rustled in the gentle breeze, fluttering under a three-quarter moon. Our back porch light beckoned me with its dangerous welcome. I had to pull myself away from its seductive light, from the glowing sizzling death. I flew around the small creatures haunted by its brilliance and saw their desperate attempts to know its mysteries. I struggled into the shadows of the porch swing, and, after touching what was human-made, I folded my wings back into myself and stepped into my skin. I looked for my robe. I'd left it on the porch chair. I shrugged into it and went inside.

When I saw the moth, I knew she was a changeling. Her long antennae curved like two fangs. She flew to the house where I'd supped, not on nectar, but on the long stalk of a man's neck. I left him sleeping, neck pulsing as the wound healed over.

As a human she was no beauty, either. Mousy brown hair. Gray eyes. Pearly skin. And yet her lips were softly rounded. And her curves were exciting, pale orbs and rosy nipples, buttocks round and firm. Her skin radiated life. I inhaled, feeling lust flood my veins with heat. It had been so long since I'd felt anything, any emotion. My hands shook. I was confused. I took a deep breath and forced myself to reflect. My initial impression had been wrong: she was lovely. Not conventionally so, however. Less like a rose; more like a stone with muted colors. I watched her until she clicked the door shut.

All day I was restless. I drew the curtains across the windows. Outside it was raining, water tumbling down the streets, thrumming on my roof. Behind us, the green belt forest stretched to the Sound. The forest was drenched, petals battered by heavy rain.

When Tom woke up early, complaining of a headache, I got him a cup of coffee. He perked up after his shower and then left for work. He taught biology and botany at the community college. I was glad to see him go, since he'd been so irritable lately.

When Tom came home, he wasn't happy. There was no dinner. He used to be worried I was depressed and suggested medication or therapy. He had told me to see the doctor. And I did but they couldn't find anything wrong with me. When I'm human, I am complete and ordinary. Of course I'm tired after staying out all night, but I don't go out every night. Still, I suppose I was out more at this time of year. Late spring brings a wonder of scents and flowers.

As time passed, he passed from concern to anger. I tried my best but it wasn't good enough for him.

He looked at me as I stood up, groggy with flyaway hair. "You're a mess." He looked around. "This whole place is a mess. And where's my dinner?" He lifted his briefcase. "I'll be in my study. I have papers to grade."

I opened cans of soup and peaches. I drank the peach syrup. He curled his lip at the meal. I smiled and rubbed his neck as he ate over his desk, papers spread out. Then he ignored me as he marked the papers with red ink, so I left.

I've lived for thousands of years. Time does not pass. I pass through time. I've lived in Nineveh, in Paris, and in London when it had only thirty thousand souls.

I believe I have a soul, an essence beyond the physical world. I've had centuries to think about my existence. Yet I have not reached a conclusion. How does a life lived in millennia recognize the present as being vital to an ageless soul?

I've learned patience and it helped me as I waited for her to emerge from her house.

The pinkish flowers of a tulip tree glowed like a thousand candles. A candelabrum of a tree. I was dizzy with the smell of nectar and rushed into the petals, releasing pollen clouds. After I had my fill, I flew to a leaf to watch midnight's fountain of stars.

"You're an Owlet moth." The disembodied voice startled me. I flew up.

"Wait! I mean you no harm," he said. I hovered over a holly tree and then darted under one of its barbed leaves. He laughed.

"Clever, aren't you?"

I peeked out.

"What's your name?" He waited for my answer. "Do not fear me, I beg you. I spent many hours reading about you today. I found out that you're from the family Noctuidae and there are three thousand species of you on this continent. I suppose, however, that you comprise your own species, being half-human."

"My name is Diana." My voice was minute, even amplified through my proboscis. Only his preternatural hearing allowed him to respond.

"Goddess of the Moon!"

I hid my face under the leaf. "I'm not a goddess."

"My name is Anton." He gave a courtly bow.

"Why are you barefoot?" I asked, not knowing what to say. I blurted out the first thing that came to my mind.

"I enjoy the earth beneath my feet. The earth is the oldest being, the greatest organic life one can connect with. I'm as attracted to life as you are to your porch light."

"You saw me!" I felt nervous. "What do you want? Are you going to kill me?"

He sat down on the wet lawn. "I want to know you, not kill you. After all this time, I've found something new. You have no idea how thrilled I am. You're quite special."

I flew out and landed on a shrub closer to him. "I'm not."

"Don't be coy. There's so much to learn about you. Tell me how you came to be a moth."

I told him what I remembered. "And when there's a full moon, I'm a moth until the moon sets. I can't change back into a human even if I want to. Otherwise, I change whenever I want to." I paused. "But, really, it's almost a compulsion to change."

He nodded. "I'm always a vampire. I sleep often during the day, but my hungers drive me out at night. Usually, I dine on animal blood, but sometimes . . ." He stopped and his eyes flickered toward my house. Suddenly, I knew.

"You've been drinking my husband's blood!" That must be why he's so irritable.

Anton nodded again. "It's bitter."

I frowned. "What do you mean?"

"Your husband's blood is bitter." He shrugged. "If you want me to stop, I will."

I thought about it and was shocked that I was even considering it. My husband was a handsome man. I was attracted to his intellectual brilliance from the start. But I was beginning to think that his beauty blinded me to his inner nature. He said cruel things to me. Even so . . .

"Leave him alone."

"Fine." Anton gazed at me. "You're not happy with him."

"Yes, I am! We love each other very much."

Anton sighed quietly. The clouds moved, casting his face into shadows. When he stood up in one fluid movement, he bent toward me.

"Good night, little one."

He melted into the shadows.

The next few nights were stormy. Rain and wind, damp and cold. I didn't meet Diana but I kept a vigil of sorts. Tom disappeared into his study every evening. I stood by the window, hidden in the darkness. I saw him pull out photos from a locked drawer in his desk. They were photos of a young woman: streaked blond hair and smiling dimples. She posed playfully in a variety of undress. He spent a long time looking at the photos before grimacing and pulling piles of student papers from his briefcase.

Later that week, the weather improved. Diana ventured out. I let her feed for several minutes before I approached her.

"Hello, Diana."

She gave a mothlike screech, her wings fluttering. "Anton! You scared me!"

We spent several delightful hours talking about everything. I hadn't realized how lonely I was. I wanted to know her when she was a woman and was sadly aware of the irony. When she was human, I slept the death sleep. I knew she could appear in her human form during the night, but I sensed her fear of me and didn't press her to change. I strived to overcome all of her reservations about me. Then perhaps she would trust me. As it was, I enjoyed her excited fluttering, the sweep of wings, and the gentle breeze as she hovered around me.

Suddenly, the door banged open. Tom stood on the porch. "Diana, where are you?"

"Oh, no!" she said as she darted away. I saw her fly under the picnic table in the yard. As soon as she touched it, she changed into a woman. A second later she crawled out, naked.

"What the hell!" Tom looked at her.

"Hand me my robe. It's there by the chair."

He reached over and threw the robe. "What are you doing?"

"I . . . uh . . . just wanted to feel the air on my skin."

He looked around. "I heard a man's voice." He jumped off the steps and walked around the yard. I was hiding in the woods on the other side of the fence. He stood in the center of the yard, confused, before striding back to Diana, who sat huddled on the steps.

"Where is he?"

"There's no one here! You can see that."

Tom grabbed her shoulders. "You better not be fooling around with someone."

"Honestly, Tom. I'm alone!" She tried to stand up but he kept pressure on her.

"I know what I heard."

She shook her head. I wanted to strangle him but kept still. "Tom, I love you. Only you."

"Yeah? Well, prove it, then." He stepped back and she stood up. He took her hand and led her into the house. He gave the backyard one more glance before slamming

122

and locking the door. I tried to see into the bedroom but the curtains blocked my view. Even so, I heard the sounds. And I hated him.

🦋 Tom has changed. Or maybe I have. He's so mean. I've been thinking of leaving him. But I'm afraid. He'll tell everyone that I'm crazy. And I can understand why he thinks that. I guess it's my fault we aren't very loving anymore. We shouldn't have any secrets from each other. I'm living a double life and he must sense it. I don't want to leave him. I just want things to be the way they were in the beginning.

Maybe I should tell him about me. If he knew he'd think I was special. Anton said I am. Tom loves me, I know he does.

My thoughts go round and round. When I'm a moth, everything seems so clear. I think I'm smarter then. When I'm a woman, I'm so confused. My life doesn't make any sense.

I took a deep breath. I *had* to tell Tom about me. If he knew the real me, he would understand and love me. I knew he would.

It would be a full moon in two nights. I'd have to show him tonight when I could still change back and forth. I needed to be able to talk to him after the change.

I heard Tom laughing. It was an ugly sound. "You're crazy, Diana."

They were standing on the porch. The light was turned off but the yard was flooded with moonlight.

"It's true, Tom, really. I know it sounds crazy but I can turn into a moth."

"Yeah, right. You know, you need help."

She skipped down the steps, throwing off her bathrobe as she did so. It seemed as if she disappeared. Tom's mouth fell open.

"Diana!"

I could see her fly toward him and hear her calling his name. He could not hear her, though. He swatted at her and she fell on his shoe. Swiftly, she changed back into a woman. She stood up, naked.

Tom was speechless. She put on her robe and led him over to the picnic table. He sat down staring at her.

"How did you do that?"

"It's a long story and I want to tell you. But now you know the truth. I'm not crazy. I . . ."

He stood up abruptly. "I've been sleeping with a bug!" He took a step back. "You freak!"

"Tom!"

He ran into the house. She followed him, crying. I stood in the shadows, unsure of what to do. I could not imagine what led her to reveal her secret to him.

Tom didn't call me all day. When I called his office, he didn't pick up. I left a message for him to call me, please. But he didn't. I just wanted to tell him how life has more variety than he'd ever imagined. As a biologist, I thought he'd be fascinated.

As my husband, I thought he'd be happy to see a new side of me. How stupid can I be? It's not as if I was telling him I was a master chef in my secret life. He was right. I was a bug. An insect. I was ugly and stupid. All day, I sat on the sofa, wrapped in my quilt, crying and telling myself how dumb I was.

Then that night when he came home, everything changed. He came over to me and put his arms around me. I was so shocked I could hardly breathe.

"I'm sorry." He began. "I didn't mean to yell at you. You have to understand how weird this is."

I nodded. "I know but it's also wonderful."

"So, have you always been like this?"

I told him about my first change and how beautiful the night is. I told him how it feels to fly and the smell of nectar deep in the throat of a flower. I told him how I change and get my wings. It felt so good to share this with him.

He sat there for awhile. He looked at me. "So you just change back and forth?"

I nodded. "Except for tomorrow night. When it's a full moon, I can't change back into a human until the moon is gone."

"What happens if a bat eats you then? Do you change back into a person when the moon sets?"

"No," I shook my head. "It's not magic, Tom! If a bat eats me, I'm dead." I shuddered.

"How do you know?"

"I met another moth woman once. I only saw her for a few weeks, and then . . . I don't know what happened to her. She told me a lot."

"I don't like the thought of you being out there at night. You could get hurt." He held my hand. My heart melted. Tears came to my eyes.

"Oh, Tom." I could tell he cared.

"Tomorrow night, I'm going out with you. I won't let anything happen to you."

I snuggled closer to him and closed my eyes. "You'd do that for me?"

He nodded. "Believe me, babe, there's going to be some big changes around here."

124

"Really?"

"Trust me," he said.

He went to get ready for bed. I cleaned up the kitchen. I was determined to make my marriage work. I decided that after the full moon, I'd ask Tom to restrain me from ever leaving the house. Maybe I could stop being a moth woman. I didn't need to go out every night, as it was. If I could just stretch it to one more night inside and one more and one more. . . . As I wiped down the counters, I thought about Anton. I'd have to say good-bye to him. I'd miss him. I was surprised how much I liked talking to him. Well, that wasn't right. I needed to confide in my husband, not a relative stranger, especially a vampire!

That night we made love, and I only slipped out of bed to stand at the window. My skin itched to change, to grow wings, but I stopped myself.

I thought I saw a shadow shifting under the big tulip tree, but I wasn't sure. I let the curtain fall back and returned to bed.

The next night, I was late getting to Diana's house. The moon was full and the streets were full of crazy drugged people. I'd been looking for a quick meal, but I did not care for the blood of addicts.

When I got to her garden, I couldn't sense her presence. I wanted to talk to her. I missed her. I prowled close to Tom's window. It was the only lit room in the house. The curtain was open and he was talking on his cell.

"Hey, babe. I wanted to wish you a happy birthday." He paused. "You know I do. I told her I wanted a divorce today. It's my present to you." He paced. "Yeah, she freaked out and left. Went home to Mama." He chuckled. "You know, with all the trust money you got today, I can quit teaching now. We can party every night, baby." After a few more words that turned my stomach, he flipped the phone closed.

He started laughing. He wandered over to the wall, standing in front of a large frame. I sharpened my vision and gasped.

Butterflies and moths were pinned on display. There were labels under each specimen. A painful cry rose from my throat when I saw today's date and "Owlet Moth" under the spread wings.

The pin pierced her heart.

I smashed the window, howling in grief. Tom jumped back. I vaulted over the sill and stood in front of him. He was shaking in shock.

"Who . . ." he tried to say.

"You killed her!"

His eyes darted to the wall. "Who?" He seemed to gain some courage. His fist rose. "Look, I don't have any money. Just get out and I won't call the police."

"You killed your wife. Diana." I pointed at the moth.

125

"You're crazy!"

"I know she was a moth. I knew her in a way you'll never know." I thought of all the nights we'd talked and I'd eased my loneliness in her gentle presence. My fangs itched.

He tried to run past me, but I was too fast. I sprang and landed in front of him, baring my fangs. He yelled, his eyes wide.

"You thought you committed the perfect murder, didn't you?" I hissed. "But I have a better plan. I'm going to kill you, drain every drop of blood in your body. Then I'll drag you into the woods and let the coyotes chew on your bones and the rats eat your eyes. Nothing will be left of you, especially your murderous heart!"

He sank to his knees. I grabbed him and bit him, sucking out all the cold bitterness, drinking until I was sick of him, and his white body lay limply at my feet.

THE WIFE WHO
LIVED ON WIND

How many times can you chew air? If it is a knot of wind, I can gnaw on it a hundred times. If it is a bone of wind, I swallow it with a slice of bread so it won't get stuck in my throat.

I am the Fabulous Florentina Scaltra! Contessa of Clouds! Duchess of the Dolomites! Marquesa di Alpini! And yes, once the pride of the late Circus Imbroglione.

And I'm an ogress married to the basest human being you can imagine. He bought me from the circus for the price of a bottle of beer. I don't have green skin or warts. My skin is as pale as a toad's belly. My eyes shine like pebbles under running water. My hair is golden and curly as a snail's tail. I was billed as more beautiful than the world-famous ogress Chantilly.

My husband is no less than Mr. Banker, the man who owns the shoe store and the cobbler therein; the Cozy Inn and its inmates, the maids and cook; the hoosegow and its sole occupant, Crazy Daisy; and the bakery, whose aromas I dine on as I pass.

Mr. Banker's first wife let money slip through her fingers like water. She loved clothes and wore several outfits at one time. The shoes matched the necklace; the necklace matched the earrings; the purse matched the belt; the dress matched her eye color. She peeled off her outfits as the day wore on. She was a Russian doll of a woman, getting smaller and smaller until he kicked her out, penniless and naked.

His second wife burned holes in their bank account as she redecorated the house into a showcase of fairy-tale taste. She had sofas made of white swan feathers that captured the guests in suffocating softness. She papered the walls in red velvet and gold lamé cloth. Underfoot, she layered costly rugs woven by child slaves. She was careless with her own children and lost several among the hall of mirrors before Mr. Banker draped the glossy surfaces with scarves and kicked her out like an uncovered couch onto the curb. He hung a sign around her neck: free, as is, no delivery.

His third wife was earthy. She was a big woman, not as big as me, of course, but passable. She ate clay. She stuffed mouthfuls between her brown teeth, roared at Mr. Banker's jokes, and liked to lift her skirts like a cancan dancer when she went shopping. She was a rollicking woman with red cheeks and loose lips. She wore a gin bottle like a second nose. She had thighs that swished together when she strutted, driving Mr. Banker crazy with lust, and her breasts were like two hillocks. He would've kept her but she had a fault. A serious one. She raided his wallet every chance she could get and would bury his money in secret holes, earthen chambers of cash, no interest, and certainly not available for withdrawals.

Because she had a brain like a pebble, she couldn't find her deposits. She barely found her own tongue every day. She was as stupid as sand. He kicked her out one day after he'd spent all of his two-week vacation digging up the expanse of the manor-sized lawn. When it started raining, the holes overfilled and water spouted from them like breaching whales.

He booted her out into the rain, where she stood for two hours, mascara streaming down her cheeks, hair plastered to her skull. Finally, she gave up and threw the gin bottle into the plate glass window, shattering it into a million faux-diamond pieces. She stomped off and that was that.

No more wives, he decided. Women always wanted to spend money. They make reasons to spend it. They take and take and leave Mr. Banker with the bills. This is what he told me when he brought me home.

"I want a wife who will live on wind." And then he took me to bed.

That's *why* he finally gave in and got a wife. He's a sex addict and refuses to get counseling. He needs a wife but he doesn't want one. Therein lies a conflict. When you need what you hate and hate what you need, well, I don't have to tell you my life is brutal.

As an ogress I am used to being laughed at. *Clumsy. Oaf. Giantess. Ugly. Freak.* At the circus, I lived with the Dog-faced Woman and the Missing Link Man. We ate at the same table with the Human Cannonball and little Nelly, the world's smallest contortionist (she was billed as thirty years old, but she was really only five), and Zorba the Zebra, whose skin was dyed faithfully every Saturday night after his weekly bath.

For special clients I was shoved into the cage naked. I kept my pride and my dignity. I refused to look at the men who crowded into the tent after stuffing twenty euros inside the waistband of the three-assed man, Cheeky.

They groaned and my handler prodded me with a stick so that I turned like a lamb on a spit.

Most of the time, though, I wore a little girl's outfit. White ankle socks. A skirt of blue satin with fingerlike fringes that swayed when I walked. A white blouse that draped my breasts like whipped cream on a double-scoop sundae. I wore a blue ribbon in my hair. They wanted me to look innocent and sweet, and they wanted me to make people gasp at the incongruity of my dress and size.

They wanted to suggest corruption under the dress and depravity behind my wide blue eyes. But evil is in the eye of the customer.

I knew who I was. A virgin ogress.

Until the circus came upon hard times and I was sold in a poker game. The owner, Parii Fistpatrick, was as drunk as the Wall-eyed Woman. He should've gotten more for me, he knew that. I stood behind him, elephant chain linked around my neck, and watched him lose. He threw a fit as Mr. Banker led me away. Mr. Fistpatrick also threw a lantern, which caught the Big Top on fire, which burned down the unicorn enclosure, which caused the gored deaths of two traveling salesmen who had been visiting the pure maidens (who were quite experienced hussies, I can assure you). The fire burned down the whole shebang, leaving its denizens homeless and its animals free to terrorize the township.

I was dragged away to a different kind of cage, where I was unceremoniously deflowered.

Perhaps you're thinking I should've snapped Mr. Banker in two with my lovely hands. Or escaped.

But I ask you, where can someone of my well-known looks escape to? I couldn't blend in with the crowd in the mall or walk on my knees along Main Street. As it is, I avoid wearing heels.

Mr. Banker tells me to eat lightly. He will not have me get bigger or eat him out of house and home. He's already discovered that having an ogress for a wife is costing him. He wouldn't buy me a queen-size bed, but even a roomful of straw costs. And a simple gown to keep me decent is expensive. He says he could cover the whole table at the king's feast for that price, which is saying something, since it seats all the cousins that intermarried, breeding a palace full of slant-nosed, gawk-toothed nobles.

My bra has enough rigging to sail a fleet of ships to the New World, he says. But he likes me to wear negligees that are lacy and scant. He likes my large breasts and golden armpit hair. He buries his nose in my belly button and drinks aquavit from it until his tongue is unknotted and he's able to do his business.

Over his shoulder, I stare at the topographical ceiling. Like a map, it shows its byways to everywhere beyond the known world. There are cobwebs where the servants missed with their feather dusters, and the cobwebs are like the ropes of the trapeze artists I used to watch. There is a faint crack on the ceiling that reminds me of a lion's tooth. And I see a continent waiting to be discovered in a water stain.

After he beds me I get a special treat: a chicken leg and a glass of watered wine. On his off days, I eat wind, that lovely oleo of pollen and sun and rain and grit.

I nibble on the west wind. I sip a southerly breeze, tasting Santa Ana winds full of desert sand. I chew on hurricane fringes that smell like oranges from Seville. I suck in all the devils of a whirlwind until my brain is full of demonic ideas and I am thinking of ways to leave this life.

I'm thinking that a wife who lives on wind is a wife who knows how to fly.

I'm thinking that a flying ogress is not a contradiction of physics.

I'm thinking that a wife can befriend a former wife who just might remember where she buried *one* cache of gold since she's been in rehab. Or a wife who might reveal Mr. Banker's charge account number, which she knows better than her children's names. Or a wife that might wish to get even with a man who left her naked on the streets and who later married into the Traveling Flambeaus, those flaming sword throwers with connections to the Norse mafia.

I'm thinking that a ticket on the fortnightly zeppelin might just take me to the New World, where I hear streets are paved with gold, and all the men are ten feet tall.

I am Florentina. I'm the wife who lived on wind. And wind will not be caged.

THE DRAGONFLY'S DAUGHTER

DEDICATED TO MY DAUGHTER MAJA

One

My name is Desetnica. My mother's milk was watery as fog. Nine sons had she, all before me. I suckled gaunt breasts or my own tight knuckles. For years, there was pain in my belly and then I was cast out of home when the moon opened my bleeding. The tenth child shall roam the world until she finds her fate, said my mother, as she tossed my red shoes at my feet.

I followed a dragonfly from the rocky garden to the forest, the deep twilight woods where the sun was only a dream and salamanders hexed the woodcutters' axes. Blunt the edges became, dull as the light, and the men slunk away, casting nervous looks over their shoulders. No one would enter those woods but I.

The trees were friendly at the edge of fields, tall elms and chestnuts, pine and birch. But the farther away I walked, the smaller became the village and the sounds of laughter, the ring of the blacksmith's forge, and the snap of clothes on the lines. Deeper into the woods, the smells of baking bread and butchered lambs, the stink of night soil, the acrid odor of burnt damp wood . . . all faded into the lush scents of woodland. There were small violets and buttercups, then toadstools and morels and red caps. The blackberry bushes parted their thickets as I waded through green knots of fruit. After I passed, still following the dragonfly, the vines knitted together again, so that I was lost to the other side of kinship and orphaned into the unnamed forest. As I walked, I crushed pine needles, releasing a sweet scent. And the forest was still, without birdsong or buzz of bee.

The dragonfly had lantern-bright wings. I followed it to a clearing where a bolt-struck oak lifted its branches, gloom clinging like nests of mistletoe. There

131

I found a small house on a wagon, decorated with the moon and the stars, and painted crimson. A gypsy woman sat on the doorstep, cutting her toenails.

"And where did you come from?" I asked, amazed. Her long black hair curled around her waist; her large dark eyes regarded me with interest. "Where is the horse to pull your cart?"

"It's not where I am from that should concern you, Dragonfly's Daughter, but where you shall go."

She sat up and sipped from a tin cup. The dragonfly rested on an emerald ring she wore on her third finger. Three times did its wings quiver before it stilled.

"Why do you call me that?" I asked. She walked with an easy swagger, like a woman who had never worn underwear.

She blew on the dragonfly and it flew away. "He brought you here, wanderer, where your fate may be found."

I frowned.

"Sit. Have some tea." She knelt by a small fire and poured a dollop of tea into the tin cup. She blew on it and offered it to me, handle first.

I looked at her. The steam rose up, filling my nose with a green scent. I inhaled, letting the aroma coat the back of my throat.

"What do you smell?" she asked as she sat down on her haunches, gathering her layers of bright skirts under her bottom. Her feet were bare, her ankles tattooed with intertwining white snakes and roses. The soles were dyed with henna in patterns of dots and swirls. A small twig was stuck on the ball of one foot. It looked like a fork in the road: "Y."

I looked at her, one eyebrow raised in confusion; she nodded once to encourage me to go on. So I breathed deeply again. "I smell . . . burning air and flashes of green light." I was surprised at my words.

She smiled. "You must drink the tea. It is made from Perunika, Perun's plant. It grows only where the ground has been struck by lightning."

"Perun?" The name nudged a memory from me, the tail of a dream I could not recall. I took a hesitant sip.

"You know him. He is the Great God, Lord of Lightning." She made a sign in the air. "You shall know him, child, in all ways but one."

"I don't understand. You're talking in riddles." My head swam. My hips felt like swaying, my young nipples ached, my heart pounded. "Who are you?" Too late did I remember that Mother said never take drink from strangers.

She didn't answer me directly but whistled sharply. From the dark shadows, a white horse trotted out. She held up a hand and the horse nosed into it. She laughed, flicking away horse spit, and rubbed his nose. "This is Lord Belin."

I had never been introduced to a horse before. We had only stringy chickens and a goat with lopsided teats. I stood up and curtsied. The gypsy woman laughed again.

She stood with her hands on her hips. "At first, I thought you were the Gift, the one taken by Perun at dawn as his due. But now I see you have a different destiny." She clucked her tongue.

The horse walked over to the wagon and backed into the traces. "It is time for us to leave. The sun must go down at the edge of the world." She bent over. She pulled off the Y-shaped twig from her foot and handed it to me.

"Here. This is the Guardian rune." I took it between two fingers. She reached over and turned it upside down so that it looked like a diviner's rod. "It means you have one that watches over you." I tied it into my hair, wrapping it with long brown strands tenfold.

She leaned down and gave me a kiss on my cheek. I was too bemused to speak. I watched her as she threw the harness over the horse's broad back and cinched the belt.

"Perun would've wed you for a day and a night," she said over her shoulder as she worked. "And then . . ." She shrugged and turned back to the reins. "But your fate lies otherwise."

I came closer. The horse rolled his eye at me. I patted his neck, combing a burr out of his forelock with my fingers. He rested his head against my shoulder. I felt the hot weight of him and saw his flanks drawing in and out with each breath. There is a special joy in being close to an animal that is aware of you as a fellow creature.

I smoothed his halter as she fitted it over his ears. She did not put a bit in his mouth. I stepped back, one hand on his broad back.

"Please, Lady. What shall I do?" I was afraid. Night was coming even to this darkest woods, and the air was stilling with uneasy expectations. I shifted from one foot to the other. Truth, I wanted to go with her in that snug caravan.

She shrugged. "You will do what must be done. Now, we are off." She climbed on the horse's back, not onto the wagon's seat. "Tch! Tch!" She shook the reins, her legs straddling Lord Belin.

I stepped away as the horse pulled forward. There was no road, no cobblestones or even rude mud path. And yet, the caravan rolled, creaking and rocking, between the trees until it was swallowed up in the gloaming.

"Wait!" I called feebly, one hand outstretched. "Wait."

I huddled around the remains of the fire and shivered from fear. I had never been alone before, not I. We slept wherever we could in our two-room cottage, unrolling our sleeping mats, legs and arms interwoven like a living fence as we slept. Nine brothers have I, and one mother. Our father is dead these past five winters, his bones crushed so his spirit will not return. How we pounded for days to grind the bone meal, club and hammer, and finally, with mortar and pestle. He was plowed with barley seeds and so gave us life again.

Two

The embers glowed weakly. I added twigs and peeled bark off trees. I sat with my arms around my knees, face turned away from the fire. I did not want light-blindness, not when all around me there were rustles and mews, skitterings and chewing. Was that a tiny bone that snapped, or a twig? My eyes stared into the blackness, seeing only dim shapes of gray. Overhead, the trees were towers of night, and the stars prickled faintly.

Then I saw one darkness separate itself from the larger, and I grabbed a burning branch. The shape loomed above me. I scrabbled backward, putting the fire between us in a pathetic attempt at defense. My firebrand was, in truth, no bigger than my thumb, but it was the only weapon I had.

A man stepped into the flickering light. He was tall and broad-shouldered. He wore a kilt and, upon his head, stag antlers. I could not see his face in the darkness.

"Are you the tenth daughter?" he asked, his voice deep as a cold well. I smelled a strong, musky odor that made me back away. I waved my burning stick. Tracks of light curved like runes.

Some ancient way of knowing made me hesitate. Mother said don't talk to strangers, Desetnica. But *I* was the stranger, the cast-off girl without home or hearth.

"I am the Dragonfly's Daughter," I said. It was not a lie, exactly. It was a truth consistent with my new situation. At home, I never lied to our mother, whose back was bent under her black dress. My only lies were to a brother who teased or taunted me as I scrubbed clothes at the river while he or that brother, or that one, ran free in their games. To be sure, they had duties: pulling the plow, seeding, and harvesting, sharpening knives. But they had time for a pipe or games of cards. Chores never stopped for women.

Last year, a wandering man told us about a new god who died on a tree. But other gods died on trees or were gored by bulls during the spring ritual. Our neighbor, Liath, died so after he drank from the sacred cup and lay with Maia, the goddess also known as my friend Vesna, when she was not moonstruck. The wandering man told us many stories about this new god, and our chieftain, Kralj, decreed that woman was born to labor. Women were cursed for all time by their disobedience to God, and in the natural order of authority must offer submission to the chief and his underlings, the village men.

But we did not adopt all the new ways. And not all of the women agreed with Kralj. One of his wives was sent away, or at least we never saw her again.

This man with his rutting odor reminded me of the goats in spring or the bull and cows. I felt my inner thighs loosen and wondered if I was not old enough after all.

He came closer, his brown skin roughened from weather. His nut-brown eyes pierced mine.

"If you are not the tenth, then you owe me nothing." He tilted his head so that the antler caught the firelight along their sharp prongs. "But you are lithesome and nubile." He reached across the low flames and touched my cheek, tracing an arc along the jawline. I could not take my eyes from his. I shivered, feeling the heat between my legs. His nostrils flared. "Will you come to me freely?"

He was young and yet . . . it was his eyes that frightened me with their ancient knowledge of lust beyond my experience. Surely, I know what men and women do. Do we not all observe the sacred rites as I have told, when the Man-Bull mates with the Maia?

Not trusting my voice, I shook my head.

His shoulders were muscled, his stomach rippled. He saw me eyeing him and drew off his kilt. I would not look there.

Yet I knew its presence, felt it rise between us, a force large as life. I backed away from him, and his hand dropped from my face. Then he saw the rune twisted in my hair.

He snorted, a half-smile on his face. "It seems that I am not your fate." For a moment, he looked sad.

We stood on opposite sides of the fire. As he stepped back, I noticed he winced.

"Is . . . are you in pain?" I asked.

He nodded. "A stone is lodged in my foot."

I felt as if I should give him recompense. Even though I was a maid, I hungered to know the couplings. I was of two minds about him. He was Man in all of his naked desire. I was not yet Woman enough.

"Let me see," I said, wanting to touch him.

He sat down and lifted his foot into my lap. I was too close to the center of him. I kept my eyes away from where they wanted to look. I saw a reddened area on the heel. It was scabbed over but as I manipulated the skin, I felt a small pebble underneath.

"How did this happen?" I wondered.

"It's been there so long," he complained quietly.

"I'll need to open the scar," I said. At his curt nod, I took a stick from the fire and scraped it against a rock, sharpening it. When I turned back, my eyes strayed but the kilt lay limply over it. I tried not to sigh.

I took up his foot and probed and dug. The pebble popped out and rolled in my skirted lap. It was amber, the stone that washes up from a wild sea they say, a stone bearing bubbles or tiny insects inside. I have never seen the sea that is wider than the sky, but once a trader brought a necklace of amber worth more than all the cattle in the village.

I mopped up the blood with a corner of my skirt. Then I poured some of the tea from the tin cup the gypsy had left and mixed it with earth. I packed the wound with the mud, ripped off a length of cloth from my skirt, and bound up the injury. "This is Perun's tea," I explained. "A god's tea should heal you quickly."

All the while, the man was silent, only breathing sharply as I poked. As I tied up the bandage and checked its tautness, I suddenly felt his hand stroking my hair. I shuddered, loose with desire.

He stood up, the kilt in one hand.

"Yes," I said. I would give myself to him, this man with no name.

But he shook his head, fastening the kilt. "No, I'll not take what is dear to you. I will not take your future."

I frowned. "Speak plainly!" Would no one give me a straightforward answer?

He grunted, a sound low from his chest. It made the hair on my arms rise.

"Take this." He threw me the amber pebble. I caught it absentmindedly, having played catch with my brothers many a time. "I know who you are," he said. "And you are not mine."

My legs shook. A keening wail erupted from my throat. I felt a sudden agonizing sense of loss.

He spun around, disappearing into the woods.

I looked down and saw his footprints: four cloven hooves.

Three

Having woven the amber into a braided hank of hair, I sat back to think, leaning against a tree trunk. The sky was paler; dawn was coming. How time had passed! In the treetops I heard a bird calling, and then it flew away, a dark dot in the far sky.

Since I'd left home a day ago, I had met a wandering gypsy woman who gave me a rune, and a stag-man who gave me amber. And neither of them wanted me. They said it wasn't my fate.

I didn't understand. I'm a smart girl. The old women say so, especially Urska, the herbal woman. If I hadn't been the tenth child, I would have been her apprentice. Before I left, she shook her head sadly and said she would miss me. My brothers turned away so that I would not see their faces. I think it was because some were crying. My mother hid her face in her apron. Kralj said I must go or bring calamity upon our village. The tenth child is offered to the world, and may the gods find me pleasing, he said. The blank wooden face of our village god watched my back as I left wearing only my skirt, tunic, head scarf, and red shoes.

I lay down on the mossy ground and fell asleep.

When I awoke, my neck was stiff. I blinked the sleep away, the dreams that clung to me like cobwebs. In my dreams, I saw my mother's face when I was born, her tears and the sweat on her brow. I slipped out, bloody and mewling, into Urska's hands. I lay on a stone altar, fists bunched and legs kicking, the moon above me like a wet nurse, dripping its light into my open mouth. A flint knife wavered over me and then was gone, clattering to planked floor. Such dreams are collected like firewood by our village soothsayer, but he was not here and I would never see him again. So I sat with my chin on my fist and tried to divine their meaning.

After some time, I gave up. My stomach growled. I was used to hunger clawing at my belly. But I had not eaten since the cock crowed yesterday, and these were barren woods, ripe only with dew and mossy rocks.

I counted the types of trees: cedar, oak, walnut, pine, fir. Not one was a fruit tree, nor was it the season for harvesting. But I would have chewed a hard green apple, pips and all.

The fire was cold. I looked for the tin cup, but it was gone. The stag man's footprints were gone, too. I puzzled over it a little, but when the thought is gone, so is its shadow, as we say.

It was time to leave. Which way? I turned three times and followed my nose. The woods surrounded me, trees big and small. The oaks were so broad I doubt five men could link hands to encircle a tree. Tall ferns brushed my shoulders as I pushed my way past. There was naught else in the way of vegetation. The trees lifted their limbs high above me, and soon the ferns gave way to needle-strewn earth. I walked a springy step, breathing a piney scent. My stomach knotted and clenched. I could find no food.

And I was thirsty.

I wandered for some time, cursing my fate. To be the tenth child is to know where you came from but never know if you arrive.

The forest was quiet. I longed for the bustle of the village, the ale maker clapping wooden tankards together to announce a new brew. Or the boys calling to their cows as they herded them home. Or the girls singing as they shaped the loaves of bread, readying them for the baker. We had only one stove in the village, a beehive of heat, where braided or smooth loaves baked to a crusty perfection.

I found myself thinking too much of barley bread or tubs of goat cheese, turnips in a sauce of butter and parsley. I felt faint with hunger.

Without a path to follow, I watched where I stepped, which is why I didn't notice at first that the trees were thinning. It was a shaft of sunlight on my toes that snapped me out of my reverie.

Astonished, I looked up. I had reached the rim of the endless woods. There was a field and a brook that ran sparkling and clear, unbefouled by cattle. I ran over the roughly plowed soil, almost tripping over the clods, until I knelt on the grassy banks of the stream. I cupped water in my hands, palmful after palmful. At last, water dripping from my chin, I was sated. I rocked back on my heels and studied the landscape.

On the far end of the field there was more forest. Indeed, I was surrounded by woods as far as my eye could see. The brook ran diagonally through the field, disappearing into the tangle of trees on both ends. There was no village, no smoke rising from any distant chimney.

And still no food. I stood up, kicking at the earth. The air was fresh and the sun warmed me, but my stomach cramped from hunger.

Then I saw the dragonfly. It landed on a tuft of grass before rising to hover over the stream. It looked like a darning needle, if such had blue, veined, transparent wings. I blinked and it was gone. I whirled around, mouth open. Where had it gone? I even looked in the stream, shading my eyes from the glare of water, but all I saw were bright stones.

I drank some more water. It tasted like wild roses and grass.

When I stood up, I jumped. There was the figure of a man about ten rods from me. A rod is the length of the king's shoulder to his fingertips. Since we had never seen the king, we used Kralj's arm. But every chief was different, some short, some tall, so a rod is only a way of saying *farther than I can spit.*

The sun was in my eyes, so I couldn't see him well. No antlers, though. My fear returned. Another stranger, another man to beware.

The women in my village say that all men are capable of all evil. We only whisper that to ourselves, of course, but the men know. They say that all women are capable of driving a man to all evil.

We live in an uneasy, sometimes loving, truce. Children are born, most wanted, some not. A wife sews her man's clothes, and if she does not like him, the sleeves are somehow too short. Or the crotch of the pants cut too high.

If a man is angry with his wife, he does not knot her yarn or spit in her tea. Instead, he refuses to talk and a wedge is driven between them that splits their union like a log on the chopping block.

I waited while the man approached. I had no weapon but my wits. And so I was scared. My fingers twisted my skirt. As he neared, I squinted. On his shoulders he carried a yoke with two small baskets hanging. They swayed and bobbed as he walked up and down the rows.

"Stop!" I said when he was close enough for me to see that his hair was a tangle of leaves and vines. His bushy beard draped his chest. It was littered with grass and twigs, flecks of moss, and sprouting seeds.

He stopped.

He wore a tunic of spring green and leggings that were chestnut brown. His feet were clad in forest-green leather boots.

If he stepped closer, I would run. If he stepped closer, I could eat, for the baskets were full of fruit. Apples and pears. Plums and rose hips. My stomach growled.

He smiled. He had a sweet smile, gentle and full-lipped. Could I trust him, this tempter of another desire?

He swung the yoke down and knelt. Taking an apple out of a basket, he polished it on his sleeve and then tossed it to me. I leaned forward to grab it.

Then I paused, feeling the sweet weight of the glossy apple in my palm.

"In the old stories," I said, "men bearing gifts are full of treachery."

He nodded. "And in the new stories, women offering fruit can lead a man to sin."

"I won't offer you fruit," I promised.

"And I will not sin with you."

I bit into the apple, the juice squirting down my chin. He grinned seeing my cheeks plump up as I chewed. I ate it all, even the stem. He sat down a few arm lengths from me and took out a cluster of dark purple fruit.

"What is that?" I pointed with my chin.

"This?" His eyebrows rose in surprise. "These are grapes, the sweetest you will ever taste." He leaned forward, offering the bunch to me. I paused only a moment. Then I came close and sat down, our knees almost touching.

I took a grape and rolled it across my lower lip. It felt smooth and sunwarmed. Then I bit into it. Juice exploded in my mouth. I groaned in pleasure.

He chuckled. "I am happy to see you enjoy my fruits."

I nodded. When I swallowed, I spoke. "That was good. Thank you."

"Everything you could ever want is on this green earth." He took out a golden pear and tossed it into my lap. "Eat."

I laughed. "I was so hungry I thought I could eat a goat, but this pear will be enough."

"Tell me," he said. "Are you the tenth?"

"Why do you ask?"

"It is the price of the fruit," he said, pursing his lips coyly.

Strange, thought I. "Everyone asks me that question."

"Everyone?"

I nodded. I rolled the pear between my hands. "I will tell you the same answer I told them. I am the Dragonfly's Daughter."

He looked disappointed. His eyes were green with flecks of brown. His cheeks were rosy. "Ah," he sighed. "Then I am not your destiny."

He scratched his head. Leaves fluttered and dropped off, catching in his beard. "No, I guess not." I frowned.

"Are you fertile?" he asked, his eyes twinkling. "Your breasts look like plums and your lips are red as cherries."

I lifted my chin. "Please keep your eyes to yourself," I sniffed. "And your unseemly questions."

He spread his hands wide and shrugged. "It is only my nature."

"To be so forward?"

"To want to plow a young furrow like yours."

"You said you would not sin with me," I reminded him as I blushed.

"So I did and it is not sin to want the love of a fair woman."

Heat flooded my cheeks. As I ducked my head, my hair swung forward. He gasped. I looked at him from under my lashes.

"What is that in your hair, spring maid?" He pointed.

"It is a rune that guards me, and the stone from the hoof of the stag man."

He stroked his beard. "And yet you remain a maid?"

"Yes." I bit into the pear.

He groaned. "Watch that juice lest it drip and mingle with your sweetest nectar."

I shook my head slightly, not understanding.

"The nectar between your legs."

I threw the pear core at him, giggling in embarrassment. It hit him on the shoulder and fell to the ground. I wiped my fingers on my skirt.

He leaned closer. "Will you not take my seed and grow fruitful?"

"No!" I scooted back, returning to my senses. This man was younger than I first suspected, thinking the beard was the growth of decades, but now I could see the strong forearms and the muscled thighs in their leggings. I was aware of his maleness, the otherness that could complement me, but I was not swooning. Even with his ribald talk, I felt tameness under his tongue, and it did not excite me like the stag man had. I had no time to wonder about this, since the green man stood up.

"Then take your skirt and wide mouth out of my field," he ordered. He turned his back to me.

I was speechless. "I'm sorry if I offended you," I said finally. I would not part on bad terms with a stranger, for many have revealed themselves as gods in the old stories.

He turned around to face me. "I have asked you to lie with me, and you said no, although I would've given you food for the rest of your life . . . such as it would be." He crossed his arms across his chest. "So go, Dragonfly's Daughter, and meet your destiny."

I scowled. "Where should I go, Green Man? Back to the woods?"

He shook his head. "Go to the tree by the river."

"There is no river." But even as I said that, my eyes took in the stream that was broadening, flooding the field beyond me. I jumped back as water lapped by my feet.

The Green Man pointed. "See that tree? Go there and sit on your shadow." Not too far away, I saw a tall tree close to the riverbank.

Then he reached into the basket and pulled out a small figure woven in straw. He gave it to me, fastening it in my hair. "And take this," he added, handing me a broad leaf, "and throw it in the river. It will carry you to the tree." With that, he kissed me on the lips, a sudden assault that took my breath away. My lips trembled and once again, I felt that rush of shameless heat. I feared I didn't know myself, for how could I be so wanton?

He grinned and turned me about, swatting my bottom. "Now go."

I whirled around but he was gone. A pile of fruit nested on a hodgepodge of leaves by my feet. I looked doubtfully at the leaf in my hand. How could it carry me down the river?

I knelt by the river and tossed it in. Instantly, it widened into a leafy raft. I stepped on it gingerly and the river pulled me along, shore racing past. The tree drew nearer and I could see it was shining with white blossoms that glowed like ten thousand candles. The raft drifted toward shore and bumped gently on the riverbank. I stepped out and went toward the tree, squinting in the light.

Four

I did as he said and sat on my shadow just outside the parasol of blossoms, letting the falling petals drift onto my hair. The sun caressed my shoulders.

I was drowsy after all the tramping through woods and fear of the night. Had I slept at all? I couldn't remember. It came to me that though I'd been busy

141

walking, I'd done no work. My hands had been idle, not washing or sweeping, not digging onions or airing bedding. How many times had I dreamed of this! While I pounded the clothes on the river rock, I'd told stories in my head of princes and raging dragons. But I'd always been interrupted by brother or friend who needed this sewn or that carried up the path. I closed my eyes, happy and content.

When I opened them, my lap was a bouquet of white flowers. The sun was high overhead and my shadow was well behaved beneath me.

"Have you rested, Dragonfly's Daughter?" The pleasant voice startled me and I twisted around. Three women stood to my right, all dressed in white. One was carrying a distaff in her hand. She was fair with straight ash hair. The second woman was full-breasted, with a black cord wrapped around her waist like a belt. She had brown hair. The third woman was older, with shining gray hair. Around her waist, she had a wide belt and hanging from it on a chain was a small pair of scissors, the most cunningly wrought pair I'd ever seen. They came closer and I stood up in deference.

"Yes, madam," I replied.

The young woman spoke. "My name is Nona."

The second woman added, "And I am Pehtra."

I looked expectantly at the third. "I am Morta."

"My name is Desetnica," I said. "I'm not really the Dragonfly's Daughter." I was puzzled. How did they know I'd been called that?

"Let's sit," said Morta. We sat in a circle, our knees bent out and our ankles crossed.

Nona continued to wind thread as she talked, her fingers moving rapidly. "You have traveled far looking for your fate."

I nodded.

"And we are here to tell you what your fate is to be," said Pehtra.

Morta said, "You are the tenth child." She smiled. "You were sent from your village because you are the gods' tithing-share."

"My mother had nine and then she had me. That is true, but I don't understand."

"Every tenth is given to the gods," said Nona. "The tenth sheaf of oats, the tenth chick, the tenth bushel of peas."

I nodded. "Yes. We leave offerings by the village god, and the rest is given to Kralj, who passes it out to those with less or keeps it himself if his need is greater." Indeed, there had been rumblings on occasion that Kralj took too much. Then he would throw a feast, and all would be forgotten.

"You are the tenth, Desetnica, even in your naming. You were given to the gods and would've been sacrificed if that had been your fate."

I frowned. "I still don't understand."

"You met the Wandering Woman who carries the sun across the sky in her red wagon. Belin is the sun god's name, and if you had been chosen, he would've bedded you at dawn and burned you at midday when the sun is hottest."

My hand covered my mouth as I gasped.

"She saw you were guarded by the Dragonfly and let you go. Lord Belin thought you kind for removing the burr from his mane and blessed you with luck." Nona motioned to Pehtra, who took off her black cord and measured it against the length of thread Nona had twisted on the distaff. Their heads bent close as they murmured.

Morta took up the story. "The Wandering Woman of the Sky gave you a magic symbol, the rune that means renewal and birth, and it is also the sign of the elk or deer."

"The stag man!" My cheeks reddened with the memory.

Nona looked up. Her eyes were troubled. With the next words, I understood why.

"If you had gone to bed with Cernunnos, you would've felt wild passion. But your life would've ended at dawn as he cut out your heart with his antler." Pehtra said. "A woman's heart is never safe with a lustful man."

I ducked my head. "I felt . . ." I couldn't say it: my own lust had been intense.

Nona nodded and said, "You are discovering your womanhood, giving birth to yourself. Part of that is learning about your own wildness."

"Everything is not what I thought," I said slowly.

Pehtra wrapped her black cord once more around her waist. Morta took Nona's thread and snipped it with her scissors. There was a moment of silence before Morta spoke.

"Life has many layers of meaning, child," she said. "You took the pebble from Cernunnos's hoof, and he blessed you. He gave you the amber stone." With that, she took her scissors and cut the rune and amber from my tangled hair. She pressed the rune against my wrist, and it imprinted in my skin: a henna-red tattoo of a dragonfly. She took the strands of my hair and braided them quickly, making a necklace with the amber hanging from one end. I bent my head as she slipped it over, and the amber pendant rested against my collarbone.

I touched it gently, remembering the stag god. Then I looked at them. "What about the Green Man?"

Nona laughed. "You desired him, no?"

I shrugged my shoulders, shyly.

She nodded knowingly. "He is the god of farmers and vegetation. We could see that you longed not for him, but for the wilder man, not one who is settled in one place like a farmer. And that is good."

"Is it?"

Again she nodded. "The Green Man would've have taken you to a soft earthy bed, but later you would've been bound in a wicker cage and killed, a sacrifice for the good of the harvest." She raised her shoulders. "The Green Man is tamer but not domesticated. And you will not stay in one place, Desetnica. It is not your destiny. At least not for ten years."

"Please," I said, "help me to understand. What is my destiny, exactly?"

Morta patted me on my knee. "We are the Fates, child," she said. "Nona spins the thread for a person's life, Pehtra measures the length of the life, and I end it." She made a cutting motion with two fingers. "You are to go out into the world and meet great throngs of people. You will see how they live and their problems and joys. You will dream their stories at night. Then we will know how to order their fate."

I sat very still. "You mean that I'm to tell you how long someone will live?" I shook my head vehemently.

Nona sighed. "Don't fret. It is the way it has always been done. You are the tenth child, the tenth daughter, and given to us." She paused. "Just like your mother, Roselle GoLightly."

My mouth fell open. I half-rose, not even knowing what I was doing. "My mother!"

Pehtra nodded.

"But she never went anywhere!"

"Yes, she did," said Pehtra. "When she was young she avoided the dangers of her coming out and made it to us. We sent her to tell stories, to travel, to dream."

"My mother?" I was incredulous. I couldn't believe it. "She is old and . . ." *Worn out,* is what I was thinking but did not say. I couldn't imagine her beyond the confines of field and hearth.

"She was young once," Nona said gently, "like you. And when her wandering time was done, she found your father and loved him. She had nine sons and hoped for a tenth. She feared for a daughter. She knew your fate: to be sacrificed by a god after moments of pleasure, or to become a storyteller."

"But . . ." I stuttered. "I don't know any stories."

"You do," said Pehtra.

I laughed halfheartedly. "Only children's stories, like Cosy Posy or Ravel, Unravel. Or . . . the boys' favorite, The Hen who wanted to crow like a Rooster."

"You know *your* story," said Morta. "It's a start."

144

I shook my head. "My mother." I still could not believe that she had traveled the world. "So . . . did she dream our villagers' deaths?"

"No," Nona replied. "When Roselle settled down, she worked hard, bearing children, raising them, and toiling in the field. She worked herself to exhaustion so she wouldn't dream. She didn't want us to know who was sick or old or unlucky."

"So she wore herself out every day," I said slowly. I felt sorry for my mother. "And she knew this would happen to me when I left."

Morta nodded. "She hoped you would not burn or be killed. But she did not know."

I shuddered. My poor mother. I remembered her eyes that morning when I left. They were swollen and red.

"I was there when you were born," said Nona. "She had a choice then. If the midwife had cut your birth cord with a flint knife, in the old way, then you would have been free of the tenth child's blessing."

"Or curse," I said bitterly.

Nona shrugged. "To go out into the world is a blessing, Desetnica. You will see marvelous things. Your mother thought it was worth it, to give you that chance."

I hugged my knees, pouting a little. What about what I wanted?

"You will roam, spinning stories, little sister." Morta plucked the straw figure from my hair. "You will bed nine men but marry the tenth. When that happens, burn this. And your wanderlust will end."

Nine men! I bit my lip. I was shocked . . . and intrigued. Maybe this would be more exciting than marrying Proul, the butcher's son.

The sisters stood up. Nona grabbed my hand and I rose to face them.

"How will I eat? How will I get new clothes and shoes?" I asked. It was all very well to cast me out with stories, but a girl must eat!

"When you tell your stories, you will be paid in such, for few have two coins to rub together," said Pehtra. "And you will learn so many stories that you will never want!"

I stood there, thoughts racing through my mind. At last one settled. "The dragonfly! Why was it my guardian?"

Morta said, "It is a symbol of your coming to maturity. It is the power of life. Think upon this. The dragonfly is born in a casing of its own body and lives in water. Then it emerges and takes to the sky, where it flies freely. Like you, it knows a different way of being according to its time of life."

"My head is whirling," I confessed.

"Here," said Nona. She tapped the tree and a branch fell down. It was carved with runic symbols and other wondrous images: a fish, the moon, sun, the bear star, a seeing eye, and spirals. "This is the storyteller's walking stick. All will recognize you by this." She picked it up and handed it to me. I grasped it. It felt like part of me, comforting and sturdy.

"And here," said Pehtra. She tapped the amber necklace and turned it up so I could see it. Inside the amber there was a tiny dragonfly. "You will take your father's spirit with you, for his ashes drifted into the creek. The dragonfly formed its larvae from your father's bones."

"Ah!" I fingered it with the other hand. My voice trembled.

"And here." They circled me, placing their hands on the top of my head. "We give you our blessings, Desetnica GoLightly."

Their hands felt like a wreath of shining stars on my head. "Thank you, ladies."

Morta smiled. "We will meet again one day, child."

"Remember that you do sacred work," instructed Pehtra. "Death can be its own blessing."

I took a deep breath. "I do not understand my fate, but I accept it."

"And that's as it should be," said Nona. "Now, go forth and tell stories."

AUTHOR'S NOTE

We're all shape-shifters, in a way. The girl grows up to be a mother; the rugged boy becomes a balding middle-aged man wearing bifocals. Sometimes, we don't even recognize ourselves. Our physical appearance has changed as we've aged: the child with blond hair ends up with dark brown hair. But we don't change species, as Diana does in the story "The Vampire and the Moth Woman." This story, like most of the others in *Butterfly Moon*, is about perceptions and has supernatural elements. Vampires are part of pop culture now, but my family came from Sibui, Transylvania ("home of the vampires"), Romania. They were not Romanian, though, but German settlers who immigrated there centuries ago. In the late 1880s, they immigrated to Montana, once more transforming themselves and their identities. The United States was founded by immigrants who wanted to shift their loyalties from the Old World and shape their destinies in the New.

Of course, the first people in the Americas were Native. I'm half Yaqui, a nation that lives primarily in Sonora, Mexico. There is a small reservation in Arizona, but my family settled in Southern California.

The story "Raven's Moon" has a Yaqui witch as one of the main characters. Miguel isn't a traditional Yaqui witch by any means. He's a modern man who happens to be about a hundred years old, in love with Raven, a witch who has forgotten her age through the millennia. Two other stories are about Yaqui experiences. Both "White Butterflies" and "Where the Bones Are" take place in the 1500s in Mexico. European diseases destroyed whole nations, transforming cultures. Not only the old people died from smallpox but also the warriors and children. Ties to precontact ways and beliefs were lost or modified, as Christianity became an important part of Yaqui life.

I retold a Yaqui story, "Tasi'o Sewa," or "The False Beggar." My contemporary story is "A Sincere Profession." I enjoyed creating a ne'er-do-well character, Warner Reynard. His last name means "Fox" in French and is an example of the Trickster figure. In "Choices," a woman is faced with a hard decision: should she save her brother's life or her husband's? This story was originally a Yaqui tale I found in the book *Yaqui Myths and Legends* by Ruth Giddings (University of Arizona Press, 1959).

Three stories, "Belle's Gift," "Painted Lady," and "Owl Woman" have the same central character, a young girl named Belle. In the first, her parents argue and split up. Her father is part Yaqui; her mother is white. Although Belle is too young to wonder at her own identity in terms of ethnic heritage, she is trying to understand the greater mystery of marriage. Belle hangs on to words, to a vocabulary that she hopes will define and give order to the world.

In "Painted Lady," Belle is still trying to figure out where her father is. Is he dead? Did Meg kill him? Or did he leave? It's hard for a little girl to understand how he could leave her.

In "Owl Woman," Coyote also makes an appearance.

This book has many stories that have been "borrowed"—as Coyote, the great trickster, would say—from other countries. I chose the countries that represented my own heritage. In addition to the Native stories I've already mentioned, "Constellation of Angels" and "On This Earth" are both stories with Native characters.

A couple of other stories are from my European background. My Endrezze/Endrizzi family came from Fai della Paganella in the alpine region of Italy. I wanted to find an Italian fairy tale I could convert to my own perspective. I read so many I couldn't keep them straight after awhile. I finally went with a title I liked: "The Wife Who Lived on Wind." In one of the stories I'd researched there was a mean husband who wouldn't feed his wife, so she ate the wind. I had a character in my head who wouldn't go away, so I made Florentina the Ogress the wife. Like many women in abusive relationships, she plans her getaway, dreaming about traveling to the New World.

"The Dragonfly's Daughter" represents my Slovenian side. I'm one quarter Slovenian; my family came from Vinica, near the Croatian river/border. Through my great-grandfather, I'm related to their national poet Oton Župančič. Many European fairy tales have the main character go through three trials on his or her journey. Desetnica is a twelve-year-old girl who is forced out of her village due to an ancient belief.

Besides writing poetry and fiction, I'm also an artist; I work with acrylics but also make collages and jewelry. The idea for "The Snow Queen" started with a painting I did for an online art contest. It led me to write a story about a woman confused and lost in our world. Loss is another type of transforming process.

As Desetnica is ordered to "go forth and tell stories," I've spent my life telling stories—orally, in writing, or visually in my art. Desetnica is cast out of her safe, insular village to see the world and discover herself as she travels. All of us are on that journey. Matsuo Bashio said it best: "The moon and the sun are eternal travelers. Even the years wander on. A lifetime adrift in a boat or in old age leading a tired horse into the years. Every day is a journey, and the journey itself is home."

I hope *Butterfly Moon* will take you adrift into another world that challenges and transforms your perceptions, yet leads you back home to yourself.

ABOUT THE AUTHOR

Anita Endrezze is an artist as well as a writer. Her recent books include *Breaking Edges* (Red Bird Press, 2012), *Throwing Fire at the Sun, Water at the Moon* (University of Arizona Press, 2000), and *at the helm of twilight* (Broken Moon Press, 1992), which won the Bumbershoot/Weyerhaueser Award. She is the recipient of the Washington State Writers Award and a GAP award. Her work is in many anthologies and literary magazines around the world.